CURSE OF THE LAUGHING TEMPTRESS

CELESTIAL CURSE SERIES: BOOK ONE

S.Y. MOON

S.Y. MOON

CURSE OF THE LAUGHING TEMPTRESS

BOOK ONE
OF THE
CELESTIAL CURSE SERIES

Revised and Expanded Edition

First Printing: June 2021

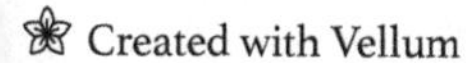

This is dedicated to the women who just want the simple things in life; good food, good sex, and good books.

So thanks husband, for providing me with those things.

And kids... you better not be reading this until you're eighteen. In which case, should you find your way into my archives.... thank you for just being you.

CONTENT WARNING

This book, as a whole, has a good mix (I feel) of humor, fun, steam and some dark themes. However, those dark themes are there.

Please be warned there are mentions of past and reoccurring abuse, stalking, murder, graphic sexual scenes as well as some other material that may make you uncomfortable.

Prologue

"They're all ugly, stupid, and have a horrible sense of fashion," the young girl said, her nose scrunching in disdain at the image of a lumbering, scrawny-haired, dull-eyed person of said description.

Her father laughed, throwing his head back and clasping his knees, and the girl instantly smiled. His voice always filled her with a profound comfort that spread like warm honey in her chest.

Wiping away a tear, her father nodded. "Ah, so is that how your mother describes humans?"

The child hugged her doll tighter. She was getting a little old for dolls, but it was given to her by the goddess Philena, who crafted the tiny porcelain masterpiece in the child's likeness with her own two hands. The small creation wore a gown of bright yellow taffeta that stood crisp and shining in the great hall of their eternal castle. Tight curls fell about her beautiful face and wide, angelic blue eyes peeped out from dark, thick lashes. Yet it was the smile that captured her heart. The two dimples punctuated light pink cheeks on alabaster skin. Yes, she adored the beauty of an uninhibited smile or laugh.

"Yes, mother says humans are horrid. I don't want to go."

"Do you believe everything your mother says?" her father asked. His voice was still teasing and his smile still bright, but even as a child she understood he was fishing for answers that she was afraid to give.

She knew better than to tell him the many ways her mother had denigrated him. Though her mother never told her outright how much she hated him, everything in the goddess's violent blue eyes, upward tilted nose, and clenched fists whenever her father was mentioned, fed the child the truth of her emotions.

"Father is funny," she'd said fondly to her mother the last time she'd seen her.

"Your father hides behind a mask child. You don't know him. I never did." The words haunted the young girl for years after. But she refused to believe them. She wouldn't believe her mother because her father loved her and gave her small trinkets and performed fantastical tricks and showered her with tight hugs and big kisses; all things her own mother never did. Without meaning to or caring, her mother had firmly pushed the child more firmly into her father's arms, and a seed of contempt festered within her, watered further by her mother's neglect.

"No. I don't believe everything she says," she whispered harshly.

"Good." Her father stood, pushing his dark blonde curls

back and yanking a strand of the child's hair as well. "Because I want you to see them for yourself. Most gods descend into their world. Your mother, despite her supposed disdain for them, goes most frequently. I'd think it was partly to get away from me."

He grimaced through his ever-present smile and she smiled brightly as well, knowing intimately the delicate game of too sore emotions that had to be concealed with laughter.

"Dad, I can't imagine humans are better company than you. You're the funniest god I know."

"Because you haven't met many people, I'm afraid. At least ones that aren't condescending elitists. But that's about to change."

The young goddess nodded, a thrill of excitement overcoming her initial hesitation. She was her father's child, and if he was asking for her trust, she'd give it wholeheartedly. She couldn't imagine any bad would come of it.

"But if humans are too ugly, I shall run screaming." She smiled, dimples of mirth on her rounded face.

"By all means." With a twinkle in his eye, he took her hand and descended the four realms into the world of mortal man: Terrin.

"THEY'RE AMAZING. The food is great. And I love their television," she said, working on her ice-cream cone as her father handed the store clerk an excessive amount of cash to cover the modest bill.

She followed her father to the cold, partially rusted metal seats outside of the ice-cream parlor and they sat in short-lived silence as they watched people walk up and down the narrow sidewalk. It was spring, and of all the places they'd visited during their time in this realm, this city with its vibrant blooming flowers and pink and white trailing blossoms that carpeted the grass and gathered in ditches along the street, was her favorite. She enjoyed watching them fall slowly to the ground as much as she enjoyed taking in all the colorful, intriguing people of the world.

Her father's low chuckle pulled her from her people-watching. She turned to face him, pressing her dimpled elbows onto the table as she watched him nod and say, "I'm glad you like them and their little quirks. You will have many things to tell your friends back home."

Her gut twisted slightly at the thought.

For them, time, especially in the human realm, moved differently. She'd been there for what must have been months, yet felt as if only a single day had passed.

"You can control that, you know." Her father had told her.

"Easier said than done. This world is weird. My body feels off. And this place makes me think I'm in the ancient past."

What they lacked in technological or magical advancements, however, they matched in eccentric charm. It was truly different from any world she'd known. And the gods had crafted many worlds in the void of space that were ten times as magical and elaborate as this land. Yet this felt like home. As she watched the people pass by, she couldn't help but envy them. These mortals, with no great burdens of power on their shoulders, no great realms to rule, wishes to grant, or elements to govern, would never know the suffering she would have to go through. They were free in their mundane natures. Free to be silly and daft, lazy and brutish. They were almost endearing in their ignorance as they moved up and down the street, unaware they were blessed by the presence of gods among them. But that was what excited her. In her realm, power and status were everything. All that mattered was how much you flaunted. She would have no freedom there. She would always have to strive to be the most powerful. The most beautiful. She'd have no choice but to be like her mother; the way her mother wanted.

"Will I grow up to be a great goddess?" she asked, licking at the melted mess of pink and blue ice cream that had trickled down her hand. She avoided his eyes but sensed them looking through her nonetheless. She wondered if, with all his godly wisdom, he really knew more than he let on. She wondered if he foresaw her destiny. She almost hoped so, so she might beg it out of him. No matter that she'd heard repeatedly that her power and all that it entailed would manifest itself in time. She didn't want to wait that long. Not with her mother's steely eyes pinning her to a future glory that she didn't think possible.

Part of her raged at the fact that none of it had even been her fault to begin with. She had been conceived in the lustful way that many lesser gods had been. She was no spark in the infinite nothingness of space and time, like the greater gods who manipulated unspeakable magic. She was instead carried for centuries within her mother's womb. Nearly as simple a beginning as a mortal child.

Though she was born a mere thirteen years prior, within her, she held centuries of existence behind her bright blue eyes. Still, she had not obtained any true power. Any meaning. Her mother resented her more for it.

"You're already a great goddess. You just have to figure out what that means to you."

His soft eyes encouraged her, almost teasing her with the

gentle way he lifted his brow and quirked his lips. Even at a time like this, he could still be insufferably juvenile.

She burst into laughter; the sound lost amongst people's chatting voices and the endless stream of cars whooshing by.

"Father, they just don't appreciate you in our world. We should stay here."

He leaned in closer, and he tugged a lock of her hair. "You like it that much? Has something in particular caught your eye?"

It was at that moment that she saw gleaming silver eyes crashing into hers from across the two-lane street. It was a man with raven black hair and a sparkling smile on heart-shaped lips. She knew he was too beautiful to be human. She scanned up and down the streets, hoping to see more of these creatures that she'd only read about in books; elusive fairytales as far as she was concerned. Regret struck her, and her eyes flew back to him, afraid that he would disappear into a shroud of magic. Her stomach dropped, heart aching in her chest when she didn't find him still standing on the empty sidewalk. A heavy longing settled inside of her. For the rest of her life, she would search for a man like that. One with dazzling dark energy behind a simmering smile.

"Yes, something's caught my eye. Lots. Let's stay. Only for a little while," she pleaded, turning to her father with wide eyes and a grin.

"Your mother won't approve," He drawled, but she already saw he was caving in.

"Please! They won't even miss us in Celora."

Her father rolled his eyes, but his lips told her she'd already won. "Fine. For twenty human years and not one decade more. I have a game I'm beholden to with the others."

"Fifty." She pouted, crossing her arms in faux irritation.

He grinned before standing and reaching out his hand for hers. He instantly let it go when he found her hand covered in sticky, melted sugar.

"We can work out the details. I'll probably leave you for a few years at a time to check in on work anyhow. I do have a job, you know."

She nodded in understanding. She'd accept anything if it meant staying here in a world that allowed her to escape the looming fate of being a god; though she'd never tell him that.

She'd barely admit it to herself that she was nothing but a runaway who feared falling short of greatness. She'd never admit that it was the moment that she saw that man across the way that she realized she could find something all her own, here in this world, where nothing made sense and yet everything came together.

She used the little bit of power she had to dispel the stickiness from her hands before she clasped her father's much larger hand and walked off down the street. In a flash of brilliance, so great that no human could perceive it, her father manipulated reality to create a fake persona she could hide behind amongst the humans.

That was the last time she would use her powers for years to come. With ease, she slipped on her mask.

"Shit!" I hissed, careening down the street with my blinker still flashing. I leaned over hazardously and reached for my charging cord as my fingers clutched my stone-dead phone. *Damn*. If I hadn't forgotten to charge it—again—I wouldn't be this late. But then, thinking back to last night's binge-fest of my favorite classic shows, I couldn't say it wasn't entirely worth it.

I screeched to a stop at the red light, plugged in the blasted device, and brought my tumbler to my lips, taking a nice, slow sip of my quick brewed coffee. I cringed, spewing the foul mixture from my mouth and onto my seat.

My gods, how had I managed to pour cream into my coffee that was so sour and putrid that it nearly curled my toes? I pinched my lips into an ugly pucker and wiped away the offensive liquid with the back of my hand.

I rolled my eyes to the heavens and wondered why no kind deity was showing me any favor today. But then, this was what rushing around half-cocked in the morning got you. And because of the teeny-tiny little fact that I was already on my last leg at work, I couldn't spare a moment to head over to the Luna Cafe for a replacement cup. And damn, did they have the best in town.

The blaring horn from behind me startled me out of my coffee-filled reverie, sending my coffee cup jerking into the air. The lid flew off, and the hot liquid spilled all over my cute little jeans and tan and white striped t-shirt.

"Ouch! Hot! Hot!" I hissed as I pulled my shirt away from my body and shook it out, desperate to cool down the fiery, rancid liquid seeping into my skin.

Damn it. Double damn. I groaned as I fumbled into my glove compartment to snatch up some thin, fast-food napkins.

The beeping increased until it strung on in one angry ribbon. I gave up, throwing the wet wad onto my seat. My cheeks burned with embarrassed indignation. With more power than necessary, my foot slammed into the pedal and I jolted forward. Of course, the disgruntled driver threw me the bird as she swerved past me. I deserved it, but that didn't stop me from throwing one right back at her on principle alone. *Jackass.* I was going through some personal issues, *thank you very much*, and I could use some sympathy. Especially today of all days.

With a sigh, I plastered a smile onto my lips, determined to keep my spirits from faltering as I sped down the road. My golden locks bounced on the breeze and I hummed along with the low thrum of music that rattled my speakers. The upbeat tune almost distracted me from the churning irritation and disappointment that I cradled in my gut. What a pathetic morning. And what a way to start my birthday.

"You're late," Mary taunted. Despite being ten years my senior, she acted more like a little kid who had nothing better to do than to wait for me to get into trouble so she could tattle—again. And you know, I wouldn't be me if I let her down.

I rolled my eyes, bit my tongue, and slid my purse from my shoulders.

I sped across the well-worn but bright alphabet rug where some of my students lay splayed out with blocks and beaten, smudge-faced dolls. I dropped my bag in my cubby and began giving good morning hugs and tidying up, an automatic habit after so many years of working there. The classroom had yet to reach full capacity and at this early morning hour, when most of the little ones were still struggling to keep their eyes open, the soft bubble of toddler voices and clanking toys was oddly soothing. Being a preschool teacher never seemed to come up as most people's dream job, but it suited me just fine.

The kids; I loved them. The co-workers on the other hand...

"Celeste, why are you late again?" came the flat, drawling voice I dreaded hearing the most.

I gulped at my boss's less than cordial greeting and steadied my nerves to confront her. I had hoped she wouldn't notice me sneaking in. Or better yet, could let me slide just this once.

I turned, taking in her scowling round face framed by blunt-cut bangs that gave her already sharp features an even harsher edge. She was shorter than me by two inches, and I stood petite myself. Yet, for all her glaring and condescending tone, she might as well have been an iron giant, and I, a damn fool, for always putting myself in her warpath.

I gave her a lopsided smile. "I'm sorry. There was an accident on the road." Not a complete lie. "And with it being my birthday..." I held my breath to see if she'd take the hint and grant me clemency.

She raised her sharp, black eyebrow, which seemed to demand an explanation as to why the celebration of my birth would matter. I had no answer for her there. Only a decent human being would give a shit about why I would like to be treated a little nicer on this day of all days. My cheeks began to ache as I struggled to maintain a mask of pleasantry. Irritation was starting to edge out my anxiety.

"I'm sorry," I repeated, ready to dismiss her as my mood warbled between annoyance and humble fear. I patted a student's fuzzy blonde head, handed him a book and pointed to the reading rug where I prayed to fucking gods, I would be able to join him soon.

"We aren't running a charity," Kathy said. "If you wanted the day off, you should have requested it. But since it's your birthday..." She shot me another scathing look. I withered under her gaze. If my intuition was worth anything, I guessed I was one more screw-up away from being fired. And though it would honestly suck to be fired on my birthday, I wouldn't waste my tears crying over it.

As much as I loved my job, I didn't really plan on being here for all of eternity. Life was too long for that.

My birthday marked more to me than just moving into a new decade. It meant that my body and soul practically vibrated in the desperate need for excitement and change. I was tired of living a life that was way too simple and unfulfilling. I was sick of acting like a fucking mouse at work because I didn't really have any idea what else I wanted to do with my life. All I knew was that I wanted *more.* I wanted life to burst open with meaning, purpose, and a shit ton of courage because I lacked that the most.

At least in one regard.

My mother's taunting voice pierced me like a banshee's scream as it played in my mind. She had no sympathy for my plight. And she remained part of the reason I had kept this lifestyle up for so long. I wanted to convince us both that I was doing the right thing in living a life she saw as useless, failing... pathetic. I'd never admit that I wondered sometimes if she was right.

I clapped my hands rhythmically, drawing the eyes of every bright-eyed baby in the class towards me.

"Ready for circle time?" I sang, walking across the room to greet a newcomer into the classroom. I took her hand and walked towards the rocking chair, gathering the other toddlers around.

I grinned as the children gave me their eager attention and babbled, some already singing their rendition of our morning rhymes.

"It's my birthday today, class! So why don't we sing the birthday song?" I clapped my hands rhythmically, leading the bars in an unabashed attempt at raising my spirits and celebrating the simmering waters of change and growth that bubbled under the surface.

My birthday. I had a few fantasies about today. I was much like a child who had waited all year for the one celebration they didn't have to share with the rest of the world. No. This day was all mine. It didn't matter that reality was proving to be at war with my fantasy. After all, on birthdays, magic can happen. And maybe that could happen today.

I smiled brighter. The coil of worry and agitation slowly

unraveled itself from my belly and evaporated into the air—until I glanced over at my boss.

She walked into her office that sat in the middle of the preschool like a starship control center and plopped down onto her makeshift throne, blinds halfway drawn so that she could watch me conspicuously. Speaking of magic... I threw my hands up, low at my sides, where no one would notice. My thoughts focused on my overseer as I imagined manifesting a fireball or something that would turn her to ash. When nothing happened, as I knew it wouldn't, I gulped, embarrassed, as I quickly turned away, dropping my hands and pushing away the self-righteous guilt that always ate at me when I thought of using my power. Especially when it was because of my wounded pride. My mother would do it. Not me.

My soprano voice wavered a little more than usual before I drew in a breath and, in broken key, finished with a wailing, "Happy birthday to me."

DURING MY LUNCH BREAK, I bolted from my building like the devil was at my heels. I slid into the driver's seat of my car and was greeted with sticky coffee — an unwelcome reminder of the shit-fest of this morning. My pants clung like a second skin to my thighs and I could not imagine a more horrendous feeling than sitting in that already smelly puddle of disgust for a second time.

"Good mood. Good mood," I chanted to myself. It wouldn't do to hurl my discarded coffee mug through my windshield. I'd just be out of three hundred bucks and get pissed off even more.

I took off towards the grocery store. I promised the kids

cupcakes for my birthday and they were damn well getting some. But… I had burned the homemade batch I started last night in between watching tv and making a detailed mental list of all the fun I'd get into on the much anticipated day of my birth. Now, that actually wasn't a part of my budding bad luck. I had always sucked at cooking. In any case, I didn't have time to buy any before work, so I was once again driving like a madwoman down the street towards the local grocers. My tires squealed as I pulled into a lucky parking spot out front. I jumped out of my sedan and bounded across the parking lot into the cool, air-conditioned front entrance.

Not being much of a baker myself, I'd frequented this part of the store on every cake worthy occasion. Like a treat-seeking missile, I made a beeline for the baked goods.

I was so zoned in on the bakery counter, I accidentally slammed into someone—my shoulder hammering them hard, and sending me stumbling back a step. I grunted in surprise and pain from the impact of it. But it was easy to ignore the dull ache in my arm once the sound of boxes crashing to the ground caught my attention. My purse had apparently swung around in the chaos and knocked over a pyramid size display of cookies. I gulped down obscenities that threatened to clue in the world to my string of irritating mishaps. I was not normally accident-prone and as clumsy as a baby calf, but the day was all sorts of odd already.

Seriously, what the hell was going on with me?

Kicking the cookies under a shelf, I tried to hide the evidence of my clumsiness as I power walked onwards. Hell-bent on my mission, and yeah, a little bit self-absorbed with my faltering day, I didn't even bother checking on the poor soul I might have sent sprawling to the ground—they made no protests and I didn't want the issues. I went up to the bakery counter, disappointed to find that there weren't enough treats out on display to fill the classroom quota.

I looked around and found no one in sight. I tapped my foot and craned my neck over the counter, feeling the seconds tick away. I didn't have the luxury of time, and if I was late back from lunch, Kathy would, for sure, fire me this time. I groaned, wanting to jump over the counter and help myself to whatever they had stashed in the back.

"Hello!" I called out, checking the time on my phone.

"Hello?" I called again, my voice breaking in annoyed impatience.

I swept my eyes over the bakery area again, looking for alternatives that wouldn't break the bank or make a colossal mess with rambunctious three-year-olds. Like a godsend, the large steel doors to the back of the bakery swung open and out walked a man who could turn my sour day into sweet rapture, I was for damn sure. And not just because he was carrying a stack of cupcakes in his hands.

My eyes widened in wild appreciation. I had to consciously stop myself from licking my lips.

His wide biceps rippled under his too-tight, black polo top, and his hair was slicked to the side in an edgy undercut that swept dark locks smoothly over eyes that flashed an inhuman shade of blood red. A wise woman might have seen those glowing orbs from a distance and run for the hills. I chose to rationalize that he wore fashion contacts and could be the answer to every single one of my prayers.

With cool, long strides, he approached the counter. Those searing eyes studied me for a moment before he spoke. "Can I help you with something?"

His voice was deep and smooth but carried a note of arrogance in it as though he had better things to do and better places to be. No matter that he wore a sweet little domestic apron tied around his neck and waist. That did nothing to lessen the hard edge about him that was equal parts thrilling and amusing. He looked like he'd be more at home, leaning against a brick wall on a shifty street corner, cigarettes in hand, and drugs in his back pocket. Yeah, he looked like he could easily be up to no good.

I smoothed down my hair and smiled, my pulse racing as his lip curled into a smirk. The man was just my type.

I stumbled over my words, almost forgetting why I was there or my desperate lack of time. "I, um, need some cupcakes, please. Chocolate or vanilla, whatever you've got ready to go. Now." I bit my lip as I noted the way his eyes traced my face with a simmering lust. A burning, heady feeling of nervous desire came to life under his gaze, and it concerned me as much as it excited me.

He outstretched his hands towards me. "Will these do?" His lips turned up again, just in one corner, seeming to be amused at my flustered state. My heart rate sped up faster; a near hum in my chest.

Gods, but my hands trembled, and I nearly knocked the plastic trays to the ground as I snatched them from his large, pale hands. I looked at him sideways, taking in that bad boy demeanor that he wore too well. The gleam in his eyes shouldn't have been that devious as he watched me awkwardly balance the treats in my arms. He had only handed me cupcakes, not a contract to steal my eternal soul. Yet, that devilish grin had me second-guessing myself and our situation.

"Have a good one," he said. And I *swear* to the gods, his voice sounded as if he were inviting me to his bed. I shivered and bit my lip, loving the way he affected me.

"Thank you," I grinned before I mournfully hurried

away. Gods knew I'd have loved for him to ask me out, but I'd love it even more if I could get back to work on time.

I felt the heat of his stare on my back and hoped I wouldn't trip over my own two feet as I scurried to the front of the store.

I rushed through check-out and out the automatic glass doors into the warm air of springtime noon.

Juggling my oversized purse on my shoulder—my arms filled with cupcakes and a little bottled coffee that I snatched up from the tiny fridge near check out—I walked towards the crosswalk. My car within sight, I hoped the clumsiness I woke up with this morning would lay off long enough for me to grab my keys and walk twenty feet without everything tumbling down.

In the world's greatest balancing act, I fished around for the car keys in my bag.

Too messy. Too many food wrappers and old pieces of mail in the thing. *Damn it.*

Tongue out, as if the gesture would assist me in finding the damned keys, my grip faltered. I watched in horror as the cupcakes tumbled into the crosswalk. I groaned, eyes looking to the heavens for comfort.

None found, I looked both ways, and reached into the street to collect my belongings. They were no longer pretty, but smooshed frosting was better than nothing.

My phone buzzed. *Shit.* I silenced my timer. Five minutes till lunch break was over and no way was I making it back on time. I bent back into the street when I felt someone grab a hold of my shoulders, their grip pinching my skin before I was roughly pulled against a hard chest. A scream sprang from my lips and my heart nearly leaped to my throat. I was going to die.

Chapter Two: Von

"Watch it!" I barked, pulling her up and out of the crosswalk just as an SUV sped past. With a jerk, I spun her around, pulling her warm, curvy frame against me. A small gasp left her lips as her chest collided with mine, and she grasped my shirt for leverage.

"Oh, shit! Bakery guy?" she yelled, eyes wide and confused, before turning her gaze to follow the vehicle that had almost taken her head off.

"One and the same. Nice to see you again and all, but you've got to stop crashing into people. You nearly knocked the shit out of me in the store earlier and now this," I grinned.

Her face reddened and her mouth formed a tiny "o" as realization hit her.

"The cookie disaster?" At my nod, she continued. "I'm really sorry about that. You must think I'm a real jackass. Which might well be true, but gods, if you had the day I've been having, you'd understand." Her shoulders drooped, her eyes filled with melodramatic misery, and I bit back a grin. If her day was rough now, it was going to get real wild pretty fucking soon.

"Is that right?" I encouraged, wanting to keep her talking and oblivious to the way my arms still wrapped around her; the way I was so intimately pressed against her, if I got a hard-on, she'd feel it right away.

She nodded her head in apparent exasperation, softly rubbing her body against me as she curled her fingers into the lapels of my shirt.

I shifted ever so slightly when her slender fingers grazed the exposed skin at my collarbone, and I *knew* she felt it then. I was barely holding myself back at that point. Fucking temptress. I had the mind to think she knew exactly what she was doing.

She had always been sinfully irresistible, and now she was right in front of me in a way I'd almost given up on imagining could ever happen.

But it was fucking real. Sure as sin, she stood right in my arms. Curly golden hair framed her face like a halo, and dimpled cheeks made her look as innocent as a cherub. That impish face could possibly fool me if I didn't know what a little seductress she was.

In reality, I knew a lot more about her than most. And if I had my way, I'd be getting very familiar with every sweet inch of her. Soon.

Her pretty pools of blue popped open when I pressed my hand to the small of her back, barely stopping myself from squeezing her ass. She bit her lip, her eyes instantly shifting into something part apprehension, part smolder as our gazes clashed.

Heat passed from her fingers into my skin as she slid

her hands to my bicep, and *almost* stroked me, *almost* pushed further against me. My cock twitched, tight in my jeans, and my hastily thrown together plans for what I'd say and do at our first meeting all flew out the window. Fuck handling this gently. I was not leaving until she was mine.

But, of course, nothing was that simple when it came to Celeste.

As if burned, she jumped out of my arms and twirled away, putting three feet between us.

I frowned, watching as she strolled back to the cross-walk. Her gaze drifted into the street where the cupcakes were coloring the pavement with shades of pinks and whites.

"Damn, I have to go," she moaned, tapping her foot and setting her pretty face into a scowl. "You couldn't have saved my cupcakes?" she asked, real sorrow in her voice throwing me for a loop.

Her fucking cupcakes? I grit my teeth at her ungrateful-ness, and not least of all at the fact that I had a raging boner left to deal with.

"Excuse me?" I snapped. "I haven't heard a thank you yet—"

"Thank you so much! Of course. I owe you my life!" She gave me a wry smile. "But I really needed those."

"I guess you'd like these then?" I asked her, pointing to my cart that was conveniently filled with cupcakes.

"What? You just happen to have a cart full of cupcakes?"

I admit I didn't expect her to be suspicious.

"Yeah, I work in the bakery," I lied smoothly, quirking a brow at her.

"Oh yeah," she chuckled as she threw me a sheepish smile. "Makes sense."

"You want some?" I coaxed, pushing the cart towards her.

"I couldn't," she murmured, moving closer to my cart to examine the cupcakes she was supposedly hesitant to take. "But... if you really don't mind."

"I don't, go ahead," I encouraged her, crossing my arms and watching as she picked up three packs—to replace the one tray she lost in the little accident.

Joy, written in the glow of her eyes and purse of her pink lips, reminded me of just how unexpected this interaction remained.

So did the wide-eyed, somewhat vague look in her eyes as she searched for what I assumed was her purse—which was still hanging precariously on her shoulder.

Following my eyes, she snatched the bag from around her shoulders, her cheeks burning pink.

"Here, I'll hold that for you." I motioned for her to hand me her trays and she happily obliged.

"Thanks. You're my literal hero today." *Not quite.*

With a triumphant smile, she pulled her keys from her bag and twirled them around her finger. A dimple sprang to her cheeks and she knew damn well that she was irresistible when she did that.

"Thanks again. I really appreciate it. I mean, I'd pay you, but I don't have—"

"Who's paying?" I interrupted, before I pinned her with a questioning eye. Why the fuck would I ever pay for something I could simply take?

She laughed at what she must have thought was a joke. It was a beautiful sound that was awfully full and husky for a sweet little face like that. She was fucking cute. Sexy, in a way that was totally unique to her.

I grinned while I watched her unknowingly squeeze her

breasts together as she fumbled around inside her gigantic bag.

While nothing could compare to feeling her body against mine, at least now I could watch her and memorize every detail I'd never gotten this close to seeing before.

My eyes ran over her tempting body. She was built like a number eight. All curves and cuteness under curls and dimples. Even her smell taunted me with its seductive, sweet notes. At this distance, I could smell the fruit and salt of her skin. No fear seeped from her pores that would sour her taste. And I wanted to taste her. I wanted more than just that. If I could have, I would have abducted her on the spot.

Unaware of the darkening thoughts spurring fiery blood to pulse in my veins, she turned from me.

"Alright. I'm off! Thanks again," she said, throwing me a wave over her shoulder and running to her car, stumbling a little, before diving inside and driving off. She barely stopped at the intersection before she turned right and was out of my sight.

She was right to leave in the face of a darkness that should have revolted her at our first meeting. Had she stayed, I wouldn't be able to continue the charade—I couldn't keep pretending she didn't drive me wild with want. My devilish grin melted away as I reminded myself of what this finally meant. Hell nor high water was going to stop me from getting some fucking answers from her.

I noted the rest of the cakes in the cart and the sly scoundrel in me badgered me to draw this out a bit. *She would be needing these*, I mused before I vanished; the side-walk left empty. I had plans—not one of them good. And now that I knew that whatever magic that had kept us apart had lifted, I wouldn't be hiding in the shadows any longer.

I pulled up to my tiny ranch style house with its brilliant yellow door and my face instantly stretched into a smile. To me, my home might as well have been magic. Through those doors was carefree relaxation. Tucked away inside of those four walls, I was free to reign over a lawless land where bras were optional and I had a television and spray of romance books in nearly every corner; a haven of sorts. I'd made a place for myself that even my messed up mom and overly critical boss couldn't sully. I walked over the uneven pavement of my driveway and onto the cobbled steps leading up to my front door. My yard was small — low-maintenance — and uneven patches of poorly maintained grass sprouted out every which way. Some stout, chipped garden gnomes I'd purchased at a flea market a few years back stood on tilt about the small space and added a sort of whimsical flair that made me smile. I walked along my little sidewalk, patting the big, stone gargoyle statue that had been planted firmly by my front door since I first bought this place six years ago. It had become a ritual to greet him as I bounded up the two steps to my porch and opened up the door.

Exhausted, I plopped down onto my plush, faux leather couch and clutched my phone in my hand. I couldn't believe the day I'd had. But worse still was the agitation and tinge of despair which swirled in my stomach as I thought about my approaching night. I glanced at my phone. No new messages. The pitiful feeling spread inside of me, cold and heavier still, as I swallowed down what might have been the start of tears.

I had it all planned out. The restaurant, mall, movies. I was simple. But nothing was going that smooth and easy today. Last-minute disappointment struck with all the force of a tidal wave. My friends couldn't make it. One was sick, one's babysitter bailed, one was *kind* enough not to even make an excuse—she just didn't feel like it. I grit my teeth at that. *Jackass.*

I blinked back any liquid despair that threatened to make this day even more pathetic and thought about all the good things that had happened to me. Not least of all the fact that my dad and sister had sent me well wishes from afar, which was always fun.

But not Mom. I could have gagged at my pathetic misstep into that territory. I knew she wouldn't celebrate the day I was born. Birthing a failure left little room for festivities, I supposed.

Pushing aside the stubborn loneliness and self-pity that sprang into my heart, I bounced to my feet and gulped in a huge breath. I was young, pretty, and had my whole life ahead of me. Cake, good movies, and books waited to be explored. I could celebrate *me*, all by myself. Feeling a second wind of bubbly optimism rising in my chest, I set out to make it happen.

Nothing to do, nowhere to go... I hummed a little to myself as I headed for my bedroom with a new game plan in place.

Food and Netflix. I could cry over my sorry, lonely fate a little later.

I threw off my bra, slipped into a t-shirt and pajama shorts, and tossed my throw blanket over my legs as I plopped back onto the worn, bright yellow sofa.

Humming a little birthday melody to myself, I dialed my favorite fast-food service and smiled when someone promptly answered.

"Hello, this is Teetee's Pizza. What can we get you today?"

"Hi, I would like a large cheese. Extra cheese, please," I told her, flipping through my television screen and hoping I could find something a little sappy, a little happy, a little angsty, and with maybe a little romance.

"Got it, anything else?"

"You don't happen to have a cake by chance?"

"No, sorry ma'am. No cake."

I sighed. It was worth a shot. "Okay, can I pay cash?"

"No problem," the lady said, taking down my address. "She'll be there in about thirty."

"Nice." I grinned happily, hanging up the phone and scooching down comfortably into my cushions.

My savior would soon be riding in with tonight's main event — pizza eating — and I was going to be ready.

I started a new dating reality show. That kind of thing always caught my attention. They never worked.

You can't find love in a damn house full of jerks. And you definitely needed more time than they gave you to form a genuine bond. That's just how humans seemed to work.

Who could fall in love at the drop of a dime?

Hm. My lips curled into a grin. I don't know about love, but lust could damn well happen in the blink of an eye. My thoughts instantly drifted to my brief encounter with the cute guy from earlier. Two — or three if we're counting the apparent cookie crash — chance meetings in a row must have some meaning, right? My body grew hot remembering his hands on me, his arms wrapped around my waist, not letting me go. I should have pushed him away. I should have told him he was crossing a line. But I was weak from the way I felt with him. As if his touch had seared an imprint on my skin, I felt it lingering on my body, haunting me to distraction for the rest of the day. He was out of this world sexy and alluring. And those deep cherry red eyes flashed like sirens in my minds-eye. They certainly set off a visceral warning that a wise woman might have heeded. I wasn't particularly known for being wise.

My bad boy baker. I chuckled out loud then, tucking a stray curl behind my ear as I fought to remember every fine detail about him; TV ignored. I wondered if he was covered in tattoos, or if he had some piercings I hadn't caught sight of. I licked my lips, imagining all the possibilities. He was positively delicious, delectable. My mind juggled between the need for that man, and the very real, gnawing hunger in my gut. The most pressing and easily remedied need won out. I groaned and rubbed my stomach pitifully. Where was my pizza?

As a matter of fact, the entire hour long episode had ended and still no pizza. On the verge of calling to complain, my doorbell rang.

"Yes, coming!" I called, sprinting to the door. I smoothed down my hair and threw the door open wide.

"Delivery?"

I blinked, unsure what the hell was going on.

"Small world?" I joked as I took note of the delivery guy. It was the same guy from the store. The very same, possibly tattooed bad-boy from before. My hero.

My body hummed, sparks almost leapt from my skin as thoughts of my lust from just moments before resurfaced. "You deliver pizzas too?"

"Let's just say, I like to stay busy." He smiled, slid the pizza from its case and handed it to me. The smell fogged my mind with renewed hunger. I was too ravenous to worry about this little coincidence. I threw open the box, slid out a slice and took a bite. I moaned out loud, only catching how completely awkward and obscene that must have looked and sounded until it was a bit too late. I quickly met his eyes to find that he was staring at me as though he was about to consume me the way I was tearing into this pizza. Hot pleasure pooled between my legs at the thought. If the invite should be put on the table, I don't think it would be physically possible to decline.

My skin burned with excitement and embarrassment as I imagined the possibilities.

"Uh, well, it's nice seeing you again," I said with a bashful smile. "Thanks for this. And for earlier. You saved my neck."

I gulped and blindly studied the box in my hand, realizing how true that was. Though his rough hands around me had scared the crap out of me, he stopped one hellish day from getting far worse.

He scoffed, and I drew my eyes to meet him. "You were damn clumsy," he admonished. "But you would have been alright I'm sure," he said with confidence. My mind didn't register the meaning of his words. Only that the way he crossed his arms over his chest showed a bit of his tattooed forearm peeking out against his fair skin. And the way his head tilted to the side, flashing me with hell's eyes, made my knees go weak.

I clutched the cardboard pizza box hard and hoped the sensation would ground me as I threatened to make some terrible decisions with this devious looking man. Part of me wanted to say something clever and sexy, so he'd know the thoughts running laps in my mind. But the other part of me wanted to slam the door in his face to stop myself from crossing a line no one should cross with their pizza delivery driver. Realistically, I wasn't going to bang him right then. But I did owe him my life... So a kind gesture wasn't necessarily a bad thing. I needed to repay my debt, after all.

"Well, I owe you one anyway. You, um, want some pizza?" I asked with a grin, holding out a warm, cheesy slice for him. I was joking. My life was worth a little more than a slice of pizza.

But he actually bent down and took a slow, measured bite. His long, warm tongue just barely caressed my fingers. A wet little lick tickled my fingertip. I flinched and let out a breathy groan as my body flushed with hot desire. His eyes flashed with mischief, but he didn't look away and I didn't pull away. Not yet.

"Tastes fantastic," he moaned, leaning in closer. The low grumble of his deep voice sent shivers from my palm up and through my body.

I drew my hand back slowly, unsure of what to do. I wondered if I was wrong for desperately wanting to do *him*. He smirked as if he could hear my inner thoughts, his eyes moving from my face down to my chest, where I was quickly reminded that I was braless.

Perky nipples strained against my tight, crewcut top. Skimpy pajama shorts barely covered my thick thighs.

Modesty was at war with basic horniness at this point. I fought the urge to move the pizza box over my chest and avert my eyes; or jut out the girls and entice him a bit more.

My face burned red, and I bit back a laugh at my predicament. To hoe or not to hoe. One of life's great questions.

Oh gods.

A movement from behind him caught my eye. Probably a stray cat or squirrel bounding about my yard in the increasing darkness, but it was enough to break the lust spell.

It was getting late, and I didn't know this guy from Adam. He could be dangerous. No, I *knew* he was. And the encroaching night, sending deep shimmers of dusty red sunlight to silhouette his dark hair, and brighten his frightening eyes, only punctuated my suspicions.

A thrill passed through me and I knew if I didn't get him out of my doorway, I was going to drag him through it. "The money!" I blurted out, looking about me for the cash I had already laid out on the entryway table. "Let me—"

His face soured for a moment before he offhandedly said, "It's all taken care of."

"Huh?"

"Don't worry about it," he smirked. "And hey, you might need these."

Out of pretty much thin air, the guy pulled out some cupcakes.

Okay... not weird at all.

"Oh, thank you?" I said, taking the treats out of his hands.

"Happy birthday," he said simply, before he turned and walked down my cobbled sidewalk past my stone statue and dilapidated garden gnomes.

"Wait! How'd you know it was my birthday?" I called out after him. He paused for a moment, but said nothing, disappearing down the walk.

I closed my door behind him and sat the decadent cupcakes and pizza on my coffee table.

That was strange. But who could say it was necessarily bad luck to run into a really hot guy twice in one day? Granted, the encounter left me feeling a little uneasy. After all, the bad-boy I'd been lusting after now knew where I lived. I nibbled my pizza, mulling over a growing edginess that had settled in my chest. Did he scare me? I scoffed at myself and rubbed away the lingering goosebumps our encounter left as testament on my skin. No, not really. But common sense told me he should have. Intuition told me he was capable of bad things. And I'd had enough of that today.

In fact, a lot of things were going awry with my shitty day so far, and it was becoming increasingly difficult to ignore it all.

Something was going on. That, I knew for sure. Yet, I wish I could say that's where my bizarre day ended. Little did I know, things had only just begun.

Chapter Four: Gargoyle

It would be sunset soon, a perfect time to ruin someone's life.

I'd had enough of waiting. Humans had too much shit to skirt around when it came to getting what they wanted. I was more straightforward.

Finally, there was no need to hold back; not that I had done so voluntarily. No, I knew today was going to be different the instant I got closer than a few feet to her door. The electric cloud of repellent energy that usually encased her — making an attempt to reach out to her uncomfortable at least, and excruciating at most — had disappeared. There was nothing that could stop me from getting to her now.

I knocked on her painfully bright front door. The door, the entire house, if you could call this child-sized cottage a house — shook from the force of my hand.

I would have to build her a better place. Something sturdy. Not something that I, or anyone of my kind, could tear apart in minutes.

I knocked again, a little harder this time, impatience burning inside of me. I rubbed at the imprint my knuckle left in the door.

"What the hell?" She opened the door, clothed in nothing more than a tiny shirt and shorts. Small. Too small. She was a little thin and frail, for how I typically liked my women. But fuck it. I'd widen those hips, guaranteed.

"I'm coming in."

Her mouth hung open before she scoffed. "Um, I'm sorry. Do I know you? No, wait —" She waved her hands around and shook her head, sending ringlets flying around her face. "Do you know *me*? This is my home, my castle, and no one is going to —"

She was a talker. I threw open her little glass barrier, nearly ripping it off the hinges, ducked my head, and entered her home. She scrambled inside after me.

The ceiling was higher than I thought it would be. Good.

"What the fuck? Are you serious right now?" she screamed, stumbling backward. I slammed the door shut, and she looked as skittish as a cornered rabbit.

I turned from her, looking about the place that had once been impenetrable. It was different, actually being inside. I took in her small kitchen with its topsy-turvy pile of dirty dishes on the side of the sink. Her tiny dining table where a porcelain vase of colorful pink and yellow flowers stood in the center, and loose envelopes of junk mail sprawled about as further decoration. An open box of pizza laid on her coffee table, though Celeste's scent was the only one that caught my attention. I inhaled the tantalizing blend of incense and vanilla that hung in the air. This felt like home.

"I like being here. I'll stay."

After a moment's hesitation, she made a run for the door. She was clumsy, and I was faster.

I threw out my arm, and she clung to it to stop her forward momentum. With a squeak, she pushed off and pressed herself against the wall. Her eyes were wide and wild, anger and confusion heavy in her brilliant blues. I watched with amusement. Awe, even. I had never interacted with her. All this time, she had been nothing more than an untouchable wonder. And here we were, together and alone. However, the stricken look on her too-pretty face, the tremble of her hands, the heaving of her chest, spoke louder to me than her words did. She was afraid. The realization bit into my wonder and joy, dulling the selfish amusement I'd had up until that point. Sure, I'd planned on barging my way in here, but I never planned on scaring the shit out of her. I wouldn't hurt her. She *had* to know that. Even if I was nothing but a brutish intruder to her, she could easily defend herself, I assumed.

When I had the chance, I'd explain everything to her. She'd know that in the end, I was powerless against her.

I took a step towards her and she narrowed her eyes at me before they darted frantically around the small space. She wanted to escape. To fight.

No, I wouldn't fight her, but I wouldn't let her leave either.

"Calm down."

"I will fucking kill you if you don't get out of here," she said, her voice pitched low. Threatening even in the face of danger. Backing up her threat, her hand moved like lightning as she pulled open a drawer to the small table beside her front door and brandished a puny knife. I laughed out loud. My roar thundered around the room and she shrank back, clutching the handle of her weapon harder, refusing to drop the knife that glimmered in the dull overhead light.

"Come on. I won't hurt you. You're an angry little thing, aren't you, Celeste?"

My smile dropped as the rage burned hotter in her eyes. "How do you know my fucking name, motherfucker?" she asked, surveying her surroundings. The small metal piece shook in her slender hands. She was tense, but ready.

I felt pity for the small woman in the pit of my gut as I tried to wade through my growing confusion. Of all the reactions I'd imagined, somehow, this hadn't been a scenario I envisioned on the many long nights I'd dreamt of this exact moment. She seemed to genuinely fear me. Her usually soft, jovial eyes now pierced me with hot emotions and I hesitated to make another move towards her. Perhaps I hadn't thought this completely through.

But why didn't she just attack me? What was going on in her mind? I let out a deep breath, pushing the air out with a low rumble. The thought that she needed my protection formed in my mind and made me redouble the yearning to stay by her side. I could protect her if she wouldn't protect herself.

I stepped back all the way across the living room and watched her push off of the wall in hesitation and relief.

I threw my hands up, too thrown off by her reaction to do anything but try once again to appease her. "I said I won't hurt you. I keep my word."

"If not to hurt me — though you sure as hell hurt my front door — then why are you here?"

"I don't know." I shook my head, shoving my hands into my jean pockets. "I figured you'd explain it to me. And I'm sorry, but I'm not leaving until you do." *If I had my way, not even then.*

"What?" Her voice wavered, and she seemed just as

confused at that moment as I was: As I'd been since the day I met her all those years ago.

"If I had more time. Or if I knew anything..." However, time was already up. I stepped back into the corner where the last rays of sunshine shrank below the horizon. It was the new moon, and whether she liked it or not, I was not going anywhere. I couldn't, even if I wanted to. "Celeste, I've watched you for a long time. And I don't have to anymore. Not like before. I'm here now, and I'm here to stay."

"No, you aren't," she said in disbelief.

"Oh yes, I am."

With what I assumed looked like a horrific mangle of a smile on my stone-cold lips, I stood in the corner and let the shift take hold of me. She watched me in horror, unable to look away as my wings sprang forth, my nails elongating, my body distorting. It wasn't painful. Not for someone who had done it a million times before. She cringed as I changed and allowed myself to become a permanent fixture in her home and life.

Good luck getting rid of me now.

I awoke with a colossal headache. I hadn't even drunk that much the night before. With a deep groan, I rolled out of my bed. Instead of skipping to the bathroom, per my usual regimen, I almost fell to the floor. My entire body trembled. My lower body was weak, feeling like jellyfish tentacles rather than the thick, solid legs I was used to.

I felt perspiration form on my brow. My skin burned almost feverishly. I sank back into my bed, taking a deep breath to push down the sudden nausea. I felt like shit.

And that was saying an awful lot. I never got sick. This must be pretty damn bad.

That's it, I'm calling in. Especially after last night.

Renewed fear shot from my scalp to my toenails. Almost overpowering my feelings of physical discomfort.

It had started like a dream; a fantasy even. Right at my door, like a birthday gift from the gods, was a terribly sexy man. His eyes were a piercing green, and he had a hard, masculine jaw, covered in a spray of dark stubble. His dirty blonde hair brushed against the top of his muscular shoulders and he was so tall, I had to crane my neck just to meet his eyes. He looked solid and powerful; a bear of a man that looked like he could tear down my house with a flick of his pinky. And please, if the saying went that big things come in big packages, then he was really my type of man. That was quickly flipped on its head when it all turned into a waking nightmare when he morphed into a monstrous beast.

I shivered, my heated skin suddenly felt too cold. It probably was just that, a nightmare. Nothing more. Yet, I didn't have the strength in me to go confirm it that very instant. Nope. I felt like shit as I laid on my full-size bed, looking around my modest bedroom. Blackout curtains did nothing to help me prepare for the day. I wanted to throw the blankets over my head and sleep for another five hours, or five days.

A thrill of anxiety hit me again, right in the chest.

As a matter of fact... I squinted into the corners, once again brought back to the memory of last night. The damn thing, gargoyle or whatever it was, had stood like a statue in my living room corner last night after bursting into my humble abode like a madman. On second thought, I knew a gargoyle. My ugly little friend that stood outside my front door like my good luck charm. The one guy that was around to greet me each day when I arrived home from work.

Had I imagined he turned into a sexy man and planted himself in my living room?

I burst out laughing, tears in my eyes. Man, I wished my dad was here. He'd crack a bad joke and make me feel better.

But anyhow, I probably just mixed a few too many wine coolers into my soda pop. That, combined with downing a dozen cupcakes by myself, probably didn't help me run at full capacity either.

My stomach churned at the reminder.

I drummed my finger on my thighs as I speed-dialed my workplace and waited for my boss to answer.

"Hello, Sunshine Hearts Preschool. How can I help you today?"

"Yeah, sorry, this is Celeste. I'm not feeling so well. I don't think I can make it in."

I could hear the loathing dripping through the speaker of my phone. "Well, Celeste, we don't have anyone to cover you—"

"Well, I can't come in unless you want me throwing up all over the kids," I bit out. Yes, I knew I was putting her in a tight spot, but I couldn't help that I was fucking sick. If you can imagine, I didn't take many sick days to begin with, yet she didn't consider that this must be pretty serious.

"Celeste, when you get back, we are going to have a review to discuss your behavior."

"Yeah, thanks for being so understanding. Gotta go, you know, throw up." I hung up. Not even having a single fuck to give about her anymore. I'd normally have handled that with a little more grace, but my head spun, and the grating hate in her voice made my stomach churn dangerously.

I stumbled to my bathroom, standing over my toilet just in case something decided to come hurling out of me.

Besides a little retching, nothing happened. Nausea was a worse feeling than actually just throwing up.

Gods, why was my body feeling so strange?

I looked in the mirror.

Well, despite feeling like shit, I looked good. I mean, really hot.

I leaned into the mirror, steadying myself on the counter's edge, and examined the glow illuminating my skin. The shine of my hair. No bags under my eyes. My skin was flawless. My eyes were bright and doe like. My lips were a little more pink than usual. I had woken up a fairytale princess! Wow, why had I been afraid to turn thirty?

My ego — the beautiful thing — somehow boosted my overall mood. With a bounce in my step, I brushed my teeth, ran my fingers through my curls, and headed for the kitchen.

My steps faltered mid-stride as anxiety ran its claws down my spine. I'd almost forgotten.

Taking a deep breath, I looked into the corner of the room where I was sure a beast would be waiting. Much to my immense relief, there was no trace of him.

Content to pretend that a behemoth of a man had not barged in here and turned to stone in front of my very eyes last night, I walked on. I reasoned my muscles were probably sore from the impending flu and not from trying—and failing — to carry his humongous ass out of my living room all by myself last night.

Yeah, I'd just go with that.

I had actually been prepared to call a priest if he was still there in the morning. But luck was finally emerging on my side, and I considered what might have really happened the night prior. Perhaps the pizza delivery guy had spiked my cheese. He looked up to no good showing up at my house, looking like sex on a platter. Damn deviant of a man.

I pushed both him and last night's events from my mind and took in a deep, relaxing breath.

Every second that went by had me feeling just a tiny bit

better. Coffee in my system and eggs and toast down the gullet had me feeling like a bright ball of sunshine.

With a sigh, I laid back on the sofa and smiled at the ceiling. A day off from work.

I ended up feeling guilty about calling out, as I sort of felt pretty damn good the rest of the day.

It's not like I lied, though.

I danced around my living room, almost slipping on my wood floors thanks to my holey, hot pink socks. But I was having a good time, and all the worries from earlier in the day and the day before all but vanished. Ah, somehow an unexpected day off from work just felt more relaxing than the weekend ever could.

And though I'd have to deal with Kathy's shit the next day, on a Friday no less, at least I could have today and a soon-approaching weekend to recoup.

"And if the jackass fires me..." I trailed off, knowing I had no damn recourse. Well, I could always get another job.

Maybe somewhere that appreciated me and all the love and energy I had all but thrown at the kids during my years at my job. Gods, bosses were the worst part of any job. Why couldn't my boss be a sexy man who paid me lots of money to just suck his —

The doorbell rang, jolting me out of my fantasy and making me bolt upright from where I lay splayed on my sofa. I knew it was full of shit, but I wanted to fully immerse myself in the delusion, nonetheless.

I hopped off the couch, using some long abandoned gymnastic skills from high school, to lithely make my way to the door.

Smooth as butter, I was there, opening the door, a smile plastered on my lips. As long as it wasn't a religious converter or salesman, I was going to be smiling indefinitely. It was pretty hard to keep me in a sour mood.

My smile faltered into bewilderment, and I sucked in a deep breath. There was the mailman. Clad in a nice little blue and white number. His legs looked great in it, seriously, but um...

"You again?" I squeaked.

"Small world," he said. A devious little tilt to his head told me he was just pulling my leg now.

I mean, he had to be. I couldn't hate on a guy for having three jobs and I knew I wasn't the smartest tool in the shed, but alarms went off in my head, begging me to get away from him as fast as I could.

Especially after his next words.

"Do you mind if I come in?"

So, that's how I found myself fleeing my house before it came crashing down on my head.

I wasn't sure what had happened exactly.

But my multi-careered friend had all but seduced his way into my house. Holding my hand, looking into my eyes, licking those sexy lips, and saying there was a monster in my house that he needed to help slay.

I nearly pissed my pants at hearing that. *Well shit, come on in!*

So that whole 'last night being a dream' crap was not fooling anyone, anyway. I had just assumed optimism sort of made problems go away. Whoops.

"My name is Von, by the way," he said, striding into my house as if he had lived there all his life. "Hang back here and wait on me, will you?" he said as he went searching every crevice of my house. There was not much to see in my little two-bedroom house, but he was intent on surveying every square inch.

Coming back empty-handed, he cast me a look somewhere between exasperation and blame.

"I appreciate your help, no doubt, but how are you involved in all of this?" I asked.

"That monster. The stone freak. He is most likely still here. I never thought he would become an issue. I'm helping to resolve it."

"An issue..."

"Yes, now unless you want to wake up to him on top of you tomorrow morning, help me find him."

I shivered at the thought. "Okay, I can help. Let me grab a weapon."

Being a delicate lady that lived all on her lonesome, of course, I had a shit ton of power tools in my garage.

"I wouldn't go in there if I were you," Von warned.

I ignored him, not sure what he was going on about. I needed to help. I just hoped I had something strong enough to drill through three-hundred pounds worth of stone.

I switched on the light, went into my little closet where my washer and dryer were, and almost fainted when a slew of half-dressed dead bodies fell onto the floor at my feet.

My legs wobbled, and I was suddenly in Von's arms. "Shh," he whispered in my ear. His hot breath sprang goosebumps on my neck and I leaned into his arms. "They're just sleeping."

"The hell they are!" I screamed, my voice hoarse and shaking, my mind working harder than ever before to figure out what was going on.

I knew what a dead body looked like; I had seen enough of them on tv.

And whether it was the work of the gargoyle or this sexy menace to society behind me, I had all the information I needed.

I ripped myself free from his grasp and ran out the back door of my garage. My mind reeled, heart sinking when I realized I'd be unable to grab my shoes or phone. But I was leaving with my life at least.

It was nearly sunset, and I squinted to make out my steps, afraid I'd face-plant into the dirt and make myself an easy victim.

I ran around the side of my house, padding through the thick, ankle-high grass when I heard a loud cracking sound from my roof.

I looked up in horror, my eyes fighting to find the source. I quickly made out his form; it was a creature of darkness. His back was arched, crouched over as if awaiting prey, before he stood tall, large wings expanding his silhouette against the blue and orange melded sky. The gargoyle.

My stomach clenched, my chest aching with the need to scream and the frustration that this mounting fear had made my legs so weak that I wavered, nearly falling to my knees.

"How'd you get out there?" Von asked the gargoyle, storming out of the house and following my eyes to the rooftop. He had the nerve to toss out the question so blasé it was like they'd been playing hide-and-seek!

Annoyance washed over me, dissipating the remnants of fear as if it had been nothing but morning fog. I sharpened my eyes but bit back the fountain of curses that wanted to spring forth.

I backed away instead. I was tired of this shit. I was so done. I didn't even look back when I heard that deep, frightening voice call after me or Von yell out to me as well. I didn't stop even though I could have sworn I heard my lawn being ripped to shreds and my house being demolished as they went at it for whatever reason.

They could tear each other apart for all I cared.

Please do.

Celeste shuffled through the small community park, disoriented and anxious; I could tell by the turn of her mouth — the way the typical brilliance of her smile had been replaced by a deep frown—and the usual shine of her eyes had turned to dull blue. After nearly a lifetime of watching her from afar, unseen and unknown, I felt I knew her more than I knew anyone or anything else.

She sat on the swing, moving her long legs back and forth, catching the late evening's cool breeze in her gleaming hair.

Since she was young, this simple act had comforted her, putting her at ease when she needed space away from her stresses and failures. After every perceived mess up, every bad break up, on days when she refused to cry, she'd gravitate towards the natural world, where she could clear her mind. Dramatics were not beyond her, but during her greatest moments of distress, she found her way here to sort out her thoughts in the sounds of the swishing trees and rippling waters. These same things evoked memories of the home I'd left behind. Every time she found her way here, I convinced myself that she was finding her way to me.

She dipped her head in thought, closed her eyes, and placed her hand to her heart. The gesture made my heart ache.

What I wouldn't do to comfort her. Had I not had that thought an innumerable amount of times? How many missed moments had passed between us just like this? With me watching and hoping that this time, the pain of going to her would only be half as torturous as the pain of staying away from her.

My body moved on its own, one forward step against the pavement propelling me towards her. One more time, I could try to push past that cloud of sizzling energy that kept her from my touch. That searing crackle against my skin that intensified with each step in her intoxicating direction. I was willing — had always been willing — to tear myself apart for her.

But my steps faltered. I knew this time would be as much of a waste as any attempts before. My spirit, that hope I'd lived on for years, had morphed into despondency. Trying and failing was the worst pain of all.

So instead, I watched and waited.

I could almost see the agitation as it radiated from her aura. She was so beautiful. Not just that sweet face and perfect body. She was good in spirit.

Through the years, I'd learned everything I could about what made her happy, in the hopes that I could offer her that someday. I saw the content look in her eyes and the shining dimples on her cheeks as she watched television shows about romance, ate sweets, or stayed out late with her friends. With bitter resolve, I watched her stroll hand in hand with new lovers, sharing kisses and secrets. The one secret she never told them was how she harbored an ache in her heart from constant self-doubt. Her lovers would never know, but I did. And when they left, she'd be right back here, with *me*, a wealth of inner joy keeping her from stewing in her hurt too long. It was that optimism that gave me strength. It was my only source, some days.

So too was her courage, mine. At the moment, she gave herself over to emotion, but she would not allow herself to stay down for long. Her tenacity was one of the many characteristics that made her so beautiful. Even if she didn't always recognize it in herself.

If I could ask for anything, at that moment, it was to be there beside her, supporting her, giving her a chance to use me for her happiness. If only for a moment.

I looked at my reflection in the fountain, something I did often when I forgot who I was. Of course, I could never forget *what* I was. And how, because of that, each day I stayed in Celeste's world meant risking my life. I might have been invisible to the world, and a glaring target to my enemies, but it was Celeste's eyes I needed to meet mine. I just wanted her to see me, just once. *I wished she could find me.* Before they did.

I could sense that I was not alone in this realm anymore, the stench of darkness already creeping into the air. I saw into my future and knew it was only a matter of time before I would lose the fight and, thus, the war.

But before that happened, I had one wish.

My skin hummed, my body going stiff. I felt her

approaching, her warm energy radiating from behind. But the pain wasn't there. Just her. Every fiber of my being burned in elation; every pain dissolved into nothingness. I never dreamed that my wish might just come true.

From a distance, I could see him glowing as if he wore a shroud of silver moonlight around him. In the middle of the nearly abandoned park, he stood by a fountain with his back to me, his jet black hair reflecting the lingering sunlight and making it appear as if it had gold flecks interwoven in his full mane. His tall, fit frame stood with an almost militant, rigid air that might have given him the quality of a soldier if it weren't for the soft aura around him. He was gorgeous, I knew before I could even see his face.

When he turned to me, I blinked rapidly, unprepared for the delicate features of a wonderfully beautiful man.

He was pretty. The most beautiful man I think I'd ever seen. If I didn't know better, I'd think I'd seen those deliriously gorgeous silver eyes once before.

"Hello," slipped from my lips before I could think. I smiled and took almost too eager steps towards him. I wasn't afraid of making new friends. Especially ones that looked like that. And hell, I could use the distraction.

His eyes widened, and for a second, I was afraid he'd burst into tears, or run and hide. My steps and my smile faltered. I looked behind me, afraid a damn monster was welded to my back. Perfectly possible at this point.

"You're speaking to me?" His slightly deep voice quivered as he spoke.

"Oh, yeah, I hope that's okay. My name's Celeste. I thought you looked a little upset."

"No, no!" he said, coming towards me, one step, and then two, each measured, and a little unsure, as if he were testing the waters. Finally, within arm's reach, he smiled. "I should be the one comforting you." His smile dazzled me. It was bright and nearly as glimmering as the large emerald stud he wore in his left ear.

A real pretty boy. I wanted to squeal. He was *just* my type.

But scratch that. I couldn't concern myself with sexy men when two of them were currently tearing down my house at that very moment. A house that was now riddled with dead bodies to boot.

A surge of anger jolted through me. I was screwed. Who would believe me? Well, I knew someone who would. *Shit.* I frantically checked my pockets. Right. My phone was back home. I swallowed a sob. I guess I'd just call him the old-fashioned way.

The beautiful man fiddled with the jewel in his ear, and I smiled, hoping to ease the tension. "Yeah, today has been wild. I think it's almost a full moon or something." Now *that* might explain some of this weird shit that's been going on around here.

His shoulders relaxed, and a smile crept up his face, popping a heartbreaking dimple at me. My heart fluttered. Now I understood the effect it had on people.

"It was just a new moon last night," he said.

Of course it was. I stopped myself from rolling my eyes.

"Do you feel comfortable like that? You don't have shoes on," the stranger asked. I looked down and wiggled my toes. I wasn't easily made uncomfortable.

"Yeah, I'm good. It's nice to just walk around barefoot sometimes. Good for the back muscles, you know," I joked.

He rewarded me with an even brighter smile. "My name is Sunny. Please, let me help you get home."

"Nice to meet you Sunny, but I don't know if I can go home." I sighed. I wasn't really sure of anything right now. Hell, I was unsure why this obviously glowing, not human man was here now. It was one thing after another. But did I learn my lesson? One look into his breathtaking silver eyes let me know I was going to make an unwise move. Again.

I let out a slow breath as that simmering fear that I'd lived so much of my life combating, curled like a leaden snake in my stomach. I was putting together some vague pieces of this puzzle, and I didn't like what the big picture was forming.

"We can figure this out together. Let's get you home. I promise it will be okay."

He wrapped his arm around me, and as his name implied, he felt like pure warmth.

I cuddled under his arm and let him lead me back to my place.

We walked in silence and his quiet, steady aura calmed me and allowed me a moment to catch my breath. My mind was muddied with too much emotion to make the usual small talk. Common sense aside, I was so thankful to this strange man for appearing when I so badly needed someone to help calm the anxiety that tightened my chest. Yes, jittery nerves that made my hands shake and go nearly numb. But it was honestly the fear that drew a lump of dread into my throat, making speaking near impossible at that moment.

I wasn't afraid of these men; these unexpected creatures that appeared like fantastical myths from a dream world. I'd seen worse. Hell, *I* was worse. No, this fear was not from a place that many could understand.

When no one could hurt you, and nothing could kill you, typical timidity was impossible. But what I *did* fear was what their appearance meant. I feared them the way someone fears the siren that signals an impending storm. This was an upset to everything I held dear, and I was afraid that every move I made from this moment onward would change my life forever.

I felt Sunny squeeze my arm gently, and I hid my smile as I watched my feet take each steady trudge forward.

I didn't know what to exactly expect at the end of the longest walk of my life. But I certainly never expected to lose everything that night.

My shoulders sank, and I pressed my lips into a tight grimace. *What. The. Hell.*

It was nightfall, and the orange glow of the streetlight in front of my house provided just enough clarity to take in the damage. Half my roof was lying in the grass, my front door pulled completely off its hinges, windows busted, shattered glass spread across my tiny lawn, and the gnomes, my cute little flea market gnomes, were smashed into pieces of red, white, and green. I stumbled over broken pavement and splintered wood, Sunny's arm on my forearm the only thing keeping me from falling on my face.

"I'm going to kill them. Kill. Them," I breathed out.

As I entered my suddenly dilapidated home, I came to find that not only were both Von and the gargoyle still alive but that they had seemingly taken a break from fighting just to lounge around my place and await my return.

"Why are you here?" Von seethed as soon as we walked through the door, ducking under falling plaster and wood, to join them in the living room. What was left of it anyway.

"I live here!" I yelled back before I glanced over to Sunny, whose eyes had narrowed at Von in kind.

Oh. That made more sense.

"Why are you with her?" the gargoyle asked, his baritone voice commanding my attention. I let out a sigh of relief as I took in his dark, golden locks and near shirtless physique that gleamed in the fluorescent lights of the small space. He was back to looking like a sexy, intimidating man, and I couldn't help that I was once again imagining all the things his large body could accomplish.

"I was comforting her while you two appear to have destroyed her home," Sunny snapped back. I was surprised at how his gentle voice cut through them like a solar ray. I pushed even more into his embrace as he held onto me.

Von snarled and stood to his full, towering height as if preparing to attack. "Let her go." A thrill passed through me at his command, despite myself.

"You have no claim on her," the gargoyle bellowed back, letting me know their truce, too, was only temporary. Great.

That meant that at any moment they could start tearing one another—and more importantly, my shit—apart.

"Could everyone maybe shut the fuck up so I can ask why any of you are here?" I asked, pulling out of Sunny's arms.

I would not let it happen twice. They had literally destroyed my home. The brilliant little home that I had saved up for all on my own. My meager salary barely allowed me to cover the mortgage, but it was mine, and now I had nothing but rubble at my feet.

"Why are you crying?" Gargoyle asked, furrowing his dark blonde brow as he reached towards me. I slapped his hand away.

"Because of this!" I swung my arms around the living room. "I'm so angry! You tore down half my house. I don't even..." It felt hard to form a coherent thought. I was so pissed off, I couldn't even speak.

"Okay, okay," the gargoyle said, shushing me as if my tears would destroy the world. "Don't cry. I already planned to build you a nice, big house. One much bigger and stronger than this one," he said as if that was a comfort.

"I never asked you to!" I snapped, finding one intact chair in my living room and sitting heavily on it. "I want all of you to tell me exactly why you're here so you can get the hell out!"

I looked around the room, not feeling the least bit patient.

"I've loved you for years now," Sunny said, breaking the silence. My stomach clenched and my eyes shot to his. "I've been enamored with every single part of you. I love you to the finest detail and I never thought I'd get to talk to you. This is..." His voice dropped, heavy with emotion.

My chest constricted with pity.

"I don't know you," I said. I didn't want to hurt him. But his declaration came out of left field. Well, I suppose it was just as odd as anything else that had been happening over the past two days. I hoped he wasn't some long-forgotten ex or a one-night stand I had hooked up with during my worst times.

I did sometimes make bad decisions when it came to getting some dick.

"You don't know me. But I know you. I think we all do," Sunny continued, looking around at the others for confirmation.

They offered brief nods of agreement, and that really threw me.

"This makes no sense. I know for a fact I'd remember you!" I motioned to Gargoyle. I mean, they were all gorgeous, but I'd remember climbing a tree that thick.

"It doesn't," Von agreed, arms crossed as he leaned against a nearby wall. "But it's clear that we all came here for the same purpose. We want you."

Wanted me, eh? Okay, now it was making a little sense. Very little. But it was something.

I rolled around the words a bit more. They wanted me. Heat spread throughout my body, sparking an ache between my legs. I loved the way Von had said that as if he were only stating simple facts. He had that, *I don't give a shit,* type of attitude that was rather endearing. My heart fluttered. Even with him in a half-shredded mailman uniform, his sharp, red eyes and careless hair gave him an especially irresistible edge.

The gargoyle's arms were crossed likewise. His chest jutted out in intimidation, looking ever the immovable brick house. Well, save for when my tears made him panic a few moments ago.

Sunny stood off to my side. Quiet, sweet, and somewhat anxious, if the tight look in his eyes was any indication.

All three of them were attractive and interesting in their own ways.

But these guys were also worlds different. Literally. Meaning, the connection here was vague. Why was this happening?

I wasn't sure what I should do in a situation like this. Well, what does one do when a random misfit batch of men comes barging into your life declaring their interest in you?

I had no clue. No witty remark.

All I knew was that despite myself, I was finding myself unbelievably attracted to them. Physically, at least. Given time, I think I could warm up to their personalities.

If that didn't include them destroying any more of my property. Sure, it was cute enough that they were fighting over me, but they absolutely crossed the line on this one.

I played with a loose curl that brushed against my cheek as my mind raced to figure this mess out. It was beyond me how my day could go from bad to this laughable spectacle. Yet, if it had come to this, I think I knew the only man capable of making it happen.

"Explain how you know me. Did my dad send you?"

"No. It wasn't him. I met you five years ago," Von said, not moving from his spot, holding up the wall as he spoke. "That day you fell down a flight of steps in front of the library."

My eyes widened before I let out an embarrassed chuckle. I remembered that day. I was trying to juggle a ton of books to use in my classroom. Probably not the intended use of public books, but my boss was a jerk even then and wouldn't upgrade my class' library. So there I was, being a good Samaritan, and the next thing I knew, I was falling in front of a dozen or so people.

I was sure I'd broken my ass, and I was so embarrassed that I could have died on the spot. But I was able to pick myself up, and only a few stray onlookers even acknowledged my existence.

Well, I guess add one more unseen onlooker to that.

I brushed aside a few stray tears that had squeezed past my defenses at the memory. Well, I could laugh at myself now. Everything was funnier in hindsight.

"And you?" I asked the gargoyle, the simple act of laughing somehow lifting some of the weight from my shoulders. "Your name would be helpful, by the way. Though I've taken to calling you Gargoyle at this point."

"Call me whatever you want. I saw you seventy-four moons ago. You left some human gathering. It was late. I followed you from the shadows. But I couldn't get near you."

My eyes narrowed. I had almost broken my heel running to my car that night, thinking someone was watching me. It had been my best friend's engagement party, and I didn't want to go out alone at night for a year after that. Fucking psycho.

I scoffed, throwing my hands in the air in exasperation.

"So, what's the issue exactly?" It wasn't as though I had done anything to them I could think of. Yet, they seemed to gang up on me here. Their tone was more accusatory than informative, yet I still had no idea why I was seemingly at fault.

"The problem?" Von snarled. "Do you think this is natural? Surely you aren't so dense that you can't think along the same lines as us. This has to be something beyond our control. Something magical. And I need to know what caused it."

I gasped at his outburst. "Wait, that's what this is about?"

Von barked out a dark laugh that left me shrinking back into my seat. "You're sexy as shit, but did you think I came here just to try and fuck you? I'm here for answers, sweetheart."

"Oh, wow." I leaned back further in my seat and gripped the arms of my chair. Von's crappy attitude didn't even register as the weight of his words hit me. So this wasn't just them thinking I was hot and falling head over heels. Something magical was at play. *Shit.* "So why didn't any of you just come and say hello? Ask me on a date or something? Could've gotten answers way before this."

"It's like the gargoyle said. I couldn't get near you. That's one reason why I think something else is going on here. I've tried to come into your window almost every night since then. Hasn't worked," Von said, pushing off the wall and walking my way.

"Same. I wanted to use the front door, however," Gargoyle said.

"I didn't say sneak into my house in the dead of night. I said come and talk to me," I grit out.

"The truth is, after we nearly killed each other after you left, we realized that we have both been, more or less, sharing this same interest in you. And the same inability to actually interact with you. It was almost like we were invisible to you," Von supplied.

"Some kind of force-field kept us from getting too close," Gargoyle added.

Oh no.

I turned my eyes expectantly to Sunny.

A bashful smile lit up his face. "Yes, it's true. But I was

there when you were young. Just barely entering womanhood. I never pursued you. I've just waited. In the places you love; the park. In the small garden in your backyard. I adore your flowers."

"Since I was... a kid?" I choked out.

"Yes," he blushed and nodded. "It's been a bit of a wait." His bright eyes dimmed and my heart ached for him again.

This was... a lot being thrown at me. Something magical was definitely going on here.

"Yeah, I see your point," I told them. "So you're only just now able to talk to me?"

"Seems to be that way. Only yesterday. When you bumped into me at the store, I realized how close I could get." He paused, a devilish gleam in his eyes and I blushed, knowing damn well I let him get pretty close. "So now, I'd like answers. We have a feeling you don't know what this is all about, but we need to find out how we are connected to you. And why. You can get those answers," Von told me.

I looked them over, clarifying the situation in my head. "You're right. I don't know what's going on. But... let me think." I was a little rusty with the magic stuff but I could figure out the basics at least.

"You're a beast shifter, you're a demon, and you're a fairy, right?" I asked, running my hand through my curls. Having almost zero relationship to the other realms, I was basically pulling shit from thin air, but it fit.

"You're catching on. I knew you were bright," Von told me. And though it was a sort of back-handed compliment, it made me smile.

"Well, figuring that out was easy," I said with more confidence then I had any right feeling. "Understanding what's going on is another issue entirely." I tapped my chin, mulling over the details. But I was just as lost as they were.

I did not know what to tell them.

They were like the butt of a bad joke; A gargoyle, demon, and fairy walk into a bar...

A bad joke, eh? I had no answers, but the king of bad jokes might.

Yeah, it was finally time for me to contact my dad.

Chapter Eight: Von

Celeste rose to her feet, kicking a bit of wood out of her way with a grimace. "Okay, we need to regroup. I don't really feel like lounging around here with half the walls torn out. I'm surprised the cops weren't called," she said, hands on her hips as she looked around at the devastation.

I imagined she'd throw another fit if I told her that disposing of nosy neighbors was the only way to assure the cops wouldn't become involved for some time yet.

"Sorry, some of us got carried away," Gargoyle said, shooting me a glare.

"Oh, fuck you. Who do you think is responsible for the hole in the ceiling? Those aren't my footprints in the fucking wood flooring," I scoffed. The guy was odd. Massive, for sure. He had a human form. Yet each thwack or shank I delivered was like I was hitting brick.

I'd have to fight him again, for real, someday.

If I wasn't so busy being amused by him, I'd have killed him already.

A sudden movement wiped the grin off my face. A small whiz of light and piercing sound flew towards me. I ducked, and it shot past, Sunny now its primary target. In the split second it took me to consider if I should call out a warning, he was already making his move.

His head turned to the side, and with a motion I didn't think he was capable of, he caught the lightning-fast object between his fingers. With a flick of his wrist, he hurled it back from where it had come.

"What was that?" Gargoyle boomed.

"What was what?" Celeste asked, obviously unaware of the covert little murder attempt that had just transpired.

I didn't have time to give the details, though. I sped to the back of the house, eyes sharp and wary. I looked through the open—mostly destroyed—sliding back door and could not make out the offender through the shadows. Somewhere in the shrubbery of Celeste's backyard, something waited. I could sense the eyes peering into the house. We were possibly surrounded. But Celeste was here.

Fucking shit.

I had no qualms about fighting whatsoever, but I didn't want her here to be caught in the crossfire.

"We have to go," Sunny said, grabbing ahold of Celeste's hand. My eyes narrowed at their interlocked fingers. "It's not safe here." He had the right idea, but his quick response didn't sit right with me.

"What do you mean?" she asked, as she was pulled by the not so brightly shining ball of fairy sunshine that had her hand in his. Wordlessly, he pulled her out towards the door. She snatched her purse and keys and left through the front while I lingered behind.

"Do you see anything?" Gargoyle asked, coming up behind me.

I rolled my shoulders and grit my teeth in annoyance. "No. Let's go."

What the fuck had shot into the home and why? It was full of energy, pure unadulterated power that I had to assume was hurled our way, intending to cause harm.

I hadn't been able to see the weapon clearly. I didn't know what it would have done if it had made contact. And what really pissed me off was that I didn't know who it targeted. Would someone be after Celeste?

Sunny had held the damn thing in his hands. He knew more than I did, but not for long. I'd beat answers out of him if I had to.

I stalked out the door that I had sought entrance to, in desperation, for over a decade. I didn't think I'd be leaving without answers and with an apparent threat looming over my head on top of that.

I cast a glance towards Celeste, who clumsily fiddled with her key and tried to align it with the tiny hole in her car door.

At least I wouldn't be leaving completely empty-handed.

"Why are we leaving my place again?"

"You said it was destroyed. Not suitable to stay in. Let's go," Gargoyle said, barreling his way into the passenger seat as he sank the small vehicle to the pavement.

"But my phone—"

A sudden spark flared in her now abandoned home.

"What the fuck—" she began.

"Start the fucking car," I barked. "Let's go before this turns into a shit show."

Celeste threw me a look of disgust as she started her engine, lowering the blaring radio that played her favorite mix of old-school techno. She played it every goddamn day. She was so routine it hurt. Any stalker could easily learn her schedule. I'd have to tell her that someday. I would know, after all.

"What was that flash? Did lightning just strike my house or something? I know I've been having bad luck, but shit," she huffed out, clinging to the steering wheel and shaking her curls around.

"We'll get some answers soon enough. Get ready to hit the fucking road," I told her, my patience wearing more thin than usual. I was suddenly feeling like we were all thrown into some ever-increasing mystery. For a woman whose life consisted of copious amounts of television, work, and ogling men, she was thrown straight into shit's creek today. I ignored the small part I played in that.

I stood beside her window and swept my eyes around her small yard and ominously quiet neighborhood, making sure we wouldn't be in pursuit when we fled.

"Okay. Okay. I've got no home, and I can't go to my friend's place. Not with you guys." She threw a sideways glance at the big guy who sat, knees tucked, squished like a fucking giant, beside her. "I need to get to a park, an abandoned lot, a hotel maybe?"

"Just go," I told her, as Sunny and I slid into the backseat.

"Seat belts, please," she said.

"Honey, we don't—"

"I don't care that you're impervious to car crashes. It's the law," she said with a glare.

I admit it was interesting to see Gargoyle stretch the belt out beyond its limits just to accommodate him. But he was obedient, and Celeste smiled sweetly at him. I quickly buckled, as well.

"You're worrying about the law when you've got three dead bodies in your house," I scoffed as she drove off.

She pressed on her brakes, sending me into the back of her seat before I righted myself, throwing out a curse.

"You *will* explain that," she said, pressing her foot to the gas again.

"Easy to explain," I said, rolling my shoulders and looking out the window, watching the lights blur as she sped down the highway. "How else was I supposed to get a job at those places? I don't have a resume. No job experience unless cold-blooded killer counts, and I wanted to meet you. And walking up to you in a bar just seemed a little, I don't know, cliche. I'm not a fucking mortal. I was being considerate in trying to make you feel comfortable. So I came to you like a human." *And* the shit was fun. So what, I had a dark sense of humor.

She slammed on her brakes again, and I almost cursed her out before realizing that she was stuck in traffic. She turned to me, eyes ablaze. Still hardly intimidating given her cute doll of a face, but I got the point.

"You were murdering innocent pizza drivers and mail carriers to be more human?"

"You may be good at pretending to be just like everyone else, but not everyone cares to. And I've watched enough TV with you through your blinds to know the reality of it. Humans are killers too."

"You what?!" A loud horn blaring had her cursing and turning back to the road where she sped up to make up lost space.

I smirked to myself. I knew she was going to be pissed when she found out everything. But that was a problem for another time. Right then, we had other issues.

"Get off the highway," I told her.

"Why?"

"Just listen. Off. Now," I repeated, "And lower my window."

For once, she did as I said, and I pulled myself out the window.

They were back. I could sense someone trailing us since we got on the road.

Tonight was full of surprises.

I was unsure what I was supposed to do with myself as Von crawled out my window and landed with a thud on my car roof.

"Eyes on the road," Gargoyle said gruffly, arms still crossed like he was, well, a statue. I wondered how his arms didn't cramp after a while of doing that.

"Sunny, can you see what's going on?" I asked, acutely aware of how my bright sunshine was suddenly dark and brooding back there.

He turned around, giving a small peek at the trailing roads behind us before he turned back my way.

"I can check. I'll be right back." His voice was soft and sweet and it melted my heart. That wasn't the only way he was touching me. Gods, I wanted to jump the man. I knew this was no time for it, but these sexy men were having no mercy on my libido.

Sunny was quick. Before I could tell him to be careful,

he was off, out through the window with a dim silver light trailing behind him.

A few thuds on my trunk startled me, sending my pulse racing, and made me jump halfway out of my seat. Thank god this road was not super busy. Not that it was empty, either. Gods, those two were making a complete spectacle out of everything, everywhere we went! I had half the mind to take off with god's speed and lose them in the fray. I'd still have solid G by my side, at least.

I yelped. Something hit the passenger side of the car. Hard. I jerked the wheel, my hands trembling as I righted us.

It could have been a million things, but my heart thumped, hoping it wasn't a person.

"Is a hotel close?" Gargoyle asked, pulling his arms off his chest, making me feel like maybe he was going to stuff himself out of a window at any time to join the others.

"Um, yes. I think so."

"Get there."

I nodded, before another thud overhead, and a flash of light in my eyes distracted and momentarily blinded me. The car swerved violently to the left. A scream tore through my throat, but Gargoyle's hands were on mine, righting the wheel. His large hand dwarfed mine, and I smiled, grateful and relieved for his solid presence.

"What's going on out there?" I breathed, my mind running through every possible scenario.

It would seem that something was indeed after us. Another love interest? Another mystical being, for sure. Though I hadn't seen anything, I wasn't exactly reeling in surprise over this.

I knew the territory. Where one, other-worldly being lingered, you could often find many others.

I just didn't understand the motive. Why was this happening so suddenly? The men were one thing, but the attacks? Could they be after me?

Had whatever magic that targeted my group of wannabe lovers attracted someone else to my side? Someone with less than romantic intentions?

My stomach ached. That lingering fear which sprouted up since this morning was now a raging fire, hot and painful, spreading from my gut, up into my heart.

Dad, I need you.

Up ahead, salvation was nigh.

I pressed my foot to the gas, hoping I didn't send someone flying off the hood of my car, as I made haste towards the parking lot. At the very least, we could face this adversary on fair, stationary ground.

A loud burst pierced my ears before the rear end of my car was enveloped in a sudden plume of smoke, and I lost control of the wheel. With a shriek, I felt the air leave my lungs as we headed straight for the large stone sign that signified we were close to the hotel.

I took in an even deeper breath as my door was suddenly ripped open at my side, sparkling red eyes meeting mine, as muscular arms snatched me from my seat. I rolled, tumbling against Von's body as he took the brunt of the fall against the hard pavement. *Ouch.*

A loud crash, twisting metal, and crumbling stone exploded in my ears.

As I lay pressed intimately on top of Von, I admit, I had the perverse thrill of horniness shoot through me, even at a time like that. Coming back to reality quickly, I let fear and worry take over me instead.

"Gargoyle?" I pushed myself off of Von and Sunny helped me to my feet. I walked towards my car and Sunny followed closely at my side, pulling me back when I got close to the wreckage.

"No Celeste, stay back. It could be dangerous."

"But —"

"Stay back." I heard a deep voice boom my way. I let out a breath, a smile taking over my lips.

"You need a new car," Gargoyle said as he stepped from the mangled vehicle.

I wondered if the car would just explode now. With his large frame, ripped shirt, and rippling muscles walking towards me, it would look extra cool against a backdrop of flames.

But thank the fates, that did not in fact, happen.

Instead, Sunny pulled my hand again, leading me through the parking lot and towards the hotel.

"Come on. Let's get inside."

"Are you not going to tell me what happened back there?" I asked, too comfortable to rip my hand away, but angry enough to want to. "Did you find out who it was? What, it was?"

Sunny turned me around, his hands on my shoulders as he looked me in the eyes. "Trust me. You'll be okay." His eyes were so sincere as he spoke to me, and I wanted to believe what he said. I really did.

Chapter Ten: Sunny

I rolled the vibrant green stone that hung in my ear between my fingers, hoping the nervous habit wouldn't give me away as we stepped into the lobby. The space was large and opulent with a lavish chandelier hanging overhead, and a tan, patterned floor underfoot that looked stately and posh.

A few travelers meandered around the lobby, content with life, I imagined.

These people were so unaware of the chaos that we left outside. Nor of the parade of deviants who had just strolled through their ever rotating doors.

I glanced backwards, out the revolving glass doors, knowing they would not follow us inside. As long as there were humans here, they would tread softly, so for now, I could allow myself to breathe a little easier. Only a bit.

I half-heartedly listened to Celeste introduce herself to the man at the front desk. My mind still replayed today's events on a constant loop. I had told myself long ago that I wouldn't skirt my fate. I would only be selfish for one thing, and I'd free myself once I got my one desire. But who would have predicted, in naïve inexperience, that it would be impossible to give this up now? Not her.

"My card... right." She blanched at the man as she fidgeted uselessly, patting her empty pockets. I quickly intervened.

"I have money," I told her, pulling a neatly folded wad of bills from my pocket and handing her all that I had. She could have everything I possessed. Even the most precious of my belongings if I could. If I was able. I'd give it all to her. But for now, all I could offer my precious Celeste was more secrets.

"Where'd you get that? Stole it?" Von asked, his sharp black brow rising in suspicion.

My heart sank, even as it constricted in my chest and flames of anger licked at my guilty conscience. I shifted from his heated gaze to meet Celeste's eyes and I prayed to the gods that the expression I saw glinting there was not suspicion or disgust. "Here, take it. Please," I urged. My voice was raw, nearly betraying the careful softness I worked so hard to show her.

Celeste took the money with apprehension, but she did at least accept it, as she continued to speak with the man at the front desk.

"How many rooms?" the man asked.

"One," echoed around the lobby. Bursting even from my lips before I could dare stop myself.

Celeste bowed her head, pressing her hands to her forehead in embarrassment.

But the man simply nodded, finishing up the registration. It was soon over and done, and the key to our room for the night was within Celeste's delicate hands.

As we squeezed into the small metal box that would transport us to our floor, she turned towards us and glared. "You three really think we should share a room? Or that we will be? Get it out of your mind, right this instant. I'm talking to you and my dad, and then you're leaving. All of you," she said, turning from us and walking out of the opening doors.

She sped down the hall before she threw open the door in the careless way she usually did. I followed behind as she stepped into the large space.

Fortune had shone down on us in this instance. This hotel was beautiful throughout. I was pleased to see the look of admiration on Celeste's face. Her smile widened when she laid eyes on the grandiose bed in the middle of the room. I imagined she was exhausted after how today unfolded.

"You sit down and get comfortable, Celeste. We'll be right back," Von bit out, sending Gargoyle and me an intense glare.

I sighed, positive that I knew where this conversation was headed. I knew, too, that I would lie if it meant staying here beside Celeste.

In the hallway, we stood like sentries outside of the door. Each moment with Celeste out of my sight made me anxious.

"What is the problem, Von?" I asked, hurrying the conversation along.

"Tell me what you know. Now." His voice was as hard as nails. But he didn't scare me. Nor was I intimidated by his red eyes with their demonic, vicious glow. I'd seen worse.

"What makes you think—"

"Cut the bullshit, you tinkerbell motherfucker!" he snapped, stepping closer to me. I stared him down, refusing to drop my gaze. "I know you know something. That scared ass look on your face every time we've been attacked tells me as much. But it's not that you're even scared of the attacks. You're afraid of being found out. Of Celeste finding something out." I hated Von then. Hated him for trying to ruin this moment. Perhaps some of the last moments I would have in my life to spend with Celeste. It took everything in me not to slide a blade into his chest.

My face didn't slip from its cool mask of indifference despite his intense glare. "I'm afraid for Celeste." Which was true. "I have nothing more to tell you. And if I did, if I thought I could give you any information that would make the attacks stop, I would."

His eyes, the way they examined me, sized me up and sought out every weakness, only slightly unnerved me, but not enough for me to cave. Because I knew that if I let down my guard, he wouldn't let it go and he just might arouse suspicion in Celeste. I just needed him to trust me. All of them too. Just a little while longer and I would take care of everything. I would give my entire life if it meant keeping Celeste safe.

"Come on, Von. Let's go inside," G said, breaking the tension. He at least seemed to take me at my word.

Von scoffed, shaking his head. "This isn't over. Whatever you're hiding, whatever the fuck you think you're doing so valiantly behind all of our backs, is going to come out. And if it means Celeste getting hurt in any way, rest assured, I'm ripping out your throat." He turned and knocked on the door, not sparing me a second glance.

Liar. Thief. Threat.

These bitter words he implied were acrid and haunting, as I considered just how true they were.

Celeste opened the door, a smile wide on her face as we followed her inside.

"This room is really great, Sunny. It even has a fridge." She giggled. "But, I hope you don't mind that I spent a little extra getting such a huge room. But since you were paying..." she said, walking over to the gigantic bed and bouncing on it before throwing herself back completely. She tapped her head a few times on the pillows, enjoying herself and forgetting all about us in her search for comfort.

"It's no problem," I told her, wishing I could pull her into my arms.

She sat up. A sudden scowl on her face. "But there is a problem. Could that be what you three were whispering about in the hallway?"

"We were discussing that, yeah," Von said, throwing me a seething glance.

"Well then, I should've been involved in that conversation. What was happening for the past hour while we made a run for it? Something for sure happened at my house, and in my car, and I have to be honest, I'm scared as hell that whatever it was will follow us here too. So spill. What's going on?"

I contemplated playing obtuse. But Von's eyes were already sharp as knives as he glared at me. I knew he was onto me, and I didn't want to antagonize him, lest he draw more attention to my presumed involvement.

"There seems to be something following us and they are indeed set on attacking us," I said, drawing out my words, miserable that I was forced to omit truths from her. *Lie* to her.

"Yes, I noticed. But I guess who and why is my next question," she said.

"Fuck the guessing—" Von began before I cut him off.

"We know little yet. We are still looking for answers. So until we have them, we have to be careful." I didn't look Von's way, but I didn't have to, to know his eyes were burning through me.

"Oh, gods. I don't like the sound of this. Mysterious things give me the heebie-jeebies. Especially if I'm involved in it." She leaned back on the bed, throwing her limbs wide as she looked towards the ceiling.

Worry and fear of discovery were easy to push aside as I took in her beautiful body splayed out on the white sheets. I loved looking at her like this. Long limbs and smooth skin displayed like a work of art.

"You're beautiful, Celeste," I told her, unable to hold back my admiration — my love. I knew this was forward. I knew I was a stranger to her in every way. But I had wanted to tell her that very thing for too long. How beautiful she was to me from the beginning. "And we will keep you safe. You have nothing to worry about."

She sat up, a sweet look on her face; a mixture of delight and apprehension.

"Look," she said, straightening her spine as she looked around the room. "You're all extremely attractive. And I'm definitely flattered by your affections. But trust me, this is a misunderstanding. Your feelings for me... it's probably just a cruel prank. A curse, even. Just like Von thinks. I know it. And I'm going to get to the bottom of this."

Her face was determined, set, as she crossed her legs and closed her eyes. I wanted to run to her side and hold her. I wanted to tell her that nothing was more clear than the feelings I had for her. Nothing more true. I didn't believe it was a curse. It was all but a blessing to me. But my mouth ran dry. My nerve, frail and fleeting, left me as I watched her body glow with power.

I'd only seen it a few times over the years. Her abilities mostly stayed hidden under layers of self-conscious mannerisms she learned from her encounters with others. Particularly with her mother. But I saw through it. She didn't use her powers out of fear.

She was soft-hearted and friendly for all the years that I'd known her. But she carried inside of her a bitter pride that ate at her spirit. That contradictory pride of always needing to be seen as worthy, as respected, was ingrained in her soul, but it served as her weakness. I knew what she was thinking, even if she didn't fully grasp it for what her self-deception was. If she couldn't be the best of the gods, she would be the most average of the humans. Desperation to avoid failure was the Achilles heel to her happiness. To her power. Today was the first time I'd seen her falter. That human mask was slipping. Part of me mourned for her, while the other part cheered her on.

As I witnessed her body being overcome with a soft silver light, her curls moving in the invisible winds of her powers, and her eyes opening, a glow of otherworldly divinity within them, I knew she was capable of anything.

"Dad, come here. It's your daughter. I need to talk to you, please."

In a spark of nothingness, he emerged in the middle of the room and it was impossible to ignore his origins, or hers.

I looked at the god that stood before us, a laugh in the air, a smile on his lips. His eyes sparkled in adoration as he looked down at Celeste.

"You called, sweetheart? I'm always happy to hear from you."

She bit back a smile. "Nice to see you too, Dad."

"So what seems to be the issue?" my dad asked, sinking down beside me on the plush mattress. He practically radiated cheerfulness and I have to admit, it was a little annoying. I mean, I owed him my positive disposition, so it wasn't usually an issue. I loved my dad. But right then, with my life in literal shambles? I wasn't exactly in the laughing mood.

"Dad, the joke isn't funny anymore. Stop all of this." I said, waving around at our little gathering.

"I'm sorry? What am I being accused of exactly?" He smiled. Damn that charming smile. I couldn't help but smile back.

"Dad! This reeks of your doing. It all has to be a joke, and as usual, it's not a very funny one."

"Ouch! Do you have to go straight for the jugular?" he asked, shaking his head with a light chuckle. "I am not joking, though. I never met these men before."

"Well... that... I don't know what that means. But you have to know what happened to them. These guys say they're in love with me or obsessed, at the very least. And I know it has something to do with magic. And you know how I feel about that."

My dad was well aware of the fact that I considered magical stuff a colorful little backdrop to my rather average life. Out of sight, out of mind.

It wasn't so much because I didn't want to acknowledge who, or what I was, but because I had so much to live up to in my parents' world. I wanted to carve my own path. Something forged far away from my mother's toxic version of love or success.

So this little deviation into a magical fairy tale was not welcome.

"Celeste, what makes you think this has anything to do with magic?" my dad asked with a sly smile. "I mean, who wouldn't fall in love with you? You look just like me." He finished, pinching my cheeks before I slapped his hands away.

"Not funny." It was a little funny. "Please, I'm asking for your help here." My stomach twisted in knots. Fear, my old friend, was chomping on my insides. If my dad couldn't help me, if he couldn't make everything go back to normal, I didn't know what I would do.

My father gazed at me with a rare spell of seriousness on his face. His mouth turned up into a slight smile, though his eyes remained flat as he spoke. "I'm sorry. Truly. I don't have the answers. But your mother may."

I stood to my feet, a flurry of curls and heightened dread swirling around me. "No. I won't—"

"She's your mother. You can't stop talking to her forever. You know how long that's going to be?" he smirked.

"Dad!" I crossed my arms, flopping back on the bed in agitation. I was hoping I could get more answers than this. I didn't want him to let me down now. Not now, especially if the alternative was crawling to my mom on hands and knees.

"Listen, I know how you feel," my dad said, standing. "I wouldn't send you to her if I could help it. But rather than waiting a century for me to come up with some answers, it would be best if you just went straight to the source. Believe me, you will learn what this is all about."

"Okay..." I deflated as he brushed his hand over my cheek with adoration. He was a good father. But damn him for making me do this. Why couldn't he have been the god of wisdom or something?

"Take care of my daughter. She's little more than a babe, and I trust that a hotel room filled with lustful men will not cause any issue tonight?" His damn laugh was contagious. I pressed my lips together to stop myself from falling into a peel of laughter at his highly inappropriate words.

Even my father knew that there was one thing I got from my mother, and handling myself around men was more or less one of them.

"Don't worry, we will take care of her," Gargoyle said, surprising me.

My father walked to his side and pointed his way, smiling at me. "So this guy, eh?" he shook his head in disbelief as he turned to examine the man. "Mr. Serious? I always thought a woman could appreciate a man that makes her laugh."

"I am sure I can satisfy your daughter in other ways."

A blush bloomed on my cheeks, but not from embarrassment.

"I'm certain. But only heaven knows you might be in for more trouble than even a big guy like you can handle."

My father was always a jokester. Damn him for being clued into my sex life. Gods had no boundaries.

"Thanks, Dad. If you don't mind...." I stressed, hoping this would not get any more awkward.

"I'm off. Call me if you need anything. I have friends in high places," he winked.

I shoved him, "Bye Dad."

With a shared smile, he disappeared in an echo of laughter.

"It's been a long time since we've seen him," Sunny said.

"Yeah, like two years. But that's like two minutes to him I guess," Von added while Gargoyle just stood quietly in the corner.

"Hey, stop that!" I snapped. "You don't know my dad. Just how much have you spied on me?"

"Do you really want to know?" Von asked with an arch to his sexy dark brow and a smirk on his lips.

I looked around the room. They were victims of unrequited love, and even though I had no intention of returning the favor, I felt like I owed them something for their trouble. Especially if this was my fault. Maybe I could give them my understanding and patience, at least. I let out a breath.

"Please, tell me everything."

I was prepared to find out that they had invaded my privacy. They weren't human and I couldn't expect them to abide by the laws of man. Goodness knows the gods certainly never did. But how do you prepare for peeping toms with magical abilities that liked to listen in as I did everything from crying over season finales to my private sessions of Ménage a moi?

No, no matter that I was a goddess. I would never foresee how much I'd learn from these men, or about them. And no amount of godly foresight could have ever prepared me for the journey they'd take me on to finding myself.

Chapter Twelve: Gargoyle

Like a slab of stone, I stood unmoving, just observing from beside the large hotel windows as the city lights flickered in the distance. I turned curious eyes to the ruckus outside where I noted the firetrucks and police officers swarming the sign out front where Celeste's car was smashed into pieces.

That had been too close. I had failed at protecting her.

I turned to Celeste and watched her reaction as Von wrapped up the blunt details of how he'd watched her from the shadows. Righteous anger boiled in my chest on her behalf, despite the fact that I had done similar. Not only that, but I had more than once bore witness to him peeping in on her myself, and hadn't had the sense to stop it. While I hated his presence, I had no claim to her, and I never thought he was a threat. If I couldn't break the barrier, I never assumed his scrawny ass could. On top of it, I didn't think she'd be quite this upset. After years of observation, what Celeste corrected as "stalking", I still didn't understand her completely. I grimaced at the stricken look on Celeste's face and that made me even more hesitant to admit I had been a part of Von's debauchery. I had enough of my own wrong-doings to atone for anyhow.

The little woman sat in silence. Her cheeks burned a soft pink, and a smile with no merriment was plastered on her beautiful face. She shifted on the bed, grabbing a pillow and squeezing it against her chest before tossing it to the side.

She looked around at us. Looked away from us. She teetered between rage and aloof indifference. I hadn't done half the things the other two had, yet she didn't seem pleased with any of us.

I didn't like her angry. Never planned to hurt her.

I just wanted her.

She inhaled and let out a soft sigh. Her eyes softened as she finally found words. "Unbelievable. You're all kidding me. I've left my blinds and curtains open way too much in my life. And—" her voice wavered. "And, oh gods. Even while I dated that one guy...?"

I could see the tremble of Von's hands as he spoke, his voice low. "Mark?" he nearly snarled. "Are you talking about that fucking bitch that didn't care a shit about you?"

"Yes, I mean, you saw us together? You saw *everything*?" she asked, pressing her fingertips together. The tight smile finally fell from her lips, and I frowned in confusion.

I looked at the others, noting Sunny's down-turned eyes and Von's growing, vicious anger. I'd never met the man. He was out of the picture before I met Celeste. I only knew his name from the few times I'd heard her speak of him to friends.

"Everything?" Von repeated. "Well shit Celeste, yes. Yes, I saw every fucking thing you let him get away with!" he yelled. I stood straight, uncrossing my arms as his anger sent a spike of dark energy like a lightning bolt throughout the small space. Celeste flinched, but stood her ground, grabbing bunches of the bedsheets between her straining fingers.

Her voice was low, just as dangerous as she answered him. "It was none of your business. How dare you yell at me as if I wanted that! If you were there, if you saw everything, then you know how he treated me. You know I wanted to get away but—"

"He was human. You could have."

My eyes narrowed in confusion despite my body instantly boiling in rage at what they were implying.

"I couldn't," she nearly whimpered before pushing forward with reasoning and strength in her words. "I handled it the way humans do. I have a life too, you know. A job. Friends. I can't just disappear with cosmic powers and expect that to make sense to anyone. And unlike some of us, I do care about appearing human. And I won't just throw logic out the window." She glared at Von.

"You want to know about logic? Sometimes, humans deserve to die. And he was one of them."

"He was bad, but he wasn't—" she trailed off, her voice seeming to give out as she stared down into her lap.

I wanted to yell, to intervene, and demand they tell me what happened. I had nothing to do with this, but that didn't stop the beast in my blood from wanting to murder just the same.

"He was going to kill you," Von said, voice simmering with rage. Celeste's eyes widened before squinting in what must have been confusion. She looked at Von expectantly, and I did too, hoping he told me everything I needed to know before I strangled it out of him.

"I saw him. You two had a huge fight, again, and he

stormed out of your place and went back to his house. I followed. He was wild that night. More so than usual. I was just so fucking done with it, Celeste. Done with holding myself back to spare your fucking feelings. I had sat back long enough. Waiting for you to leave. Waiting for him to stop. But I knew he wouldn't. Not that day. I couldn't enter your home until yesterday. But I could enter his. In the shadows, I watched as he went into his closet and got a gun. He got in his car and I didn't need to wait and see where he was headed. I knew, and I was there. Beside him. I had seen enough Celeste, and it was time for him to fucking pay. With him out of the home, it was so easy to get rid of his body. I did it in a few hours and no one ever knew the wiser. Not you. But you don't know how much it killed me to hear you cry over him. To hear you call his phone, ready to beg him to come back to hurt you some more. I know what it's like to want you so badly it hurts, drives me to do despicable things. But I'd never hurt you. So you can go ahead and say what I did was inhuman. That's fine with me. I wouldn't lower myself to the level of a human like that."

My head pounded, blood rushing like a raging river between my ears. With heavy, tingling limbs, I lumbered across the room and dropped beside her, bouncing her and the bed as I did so. I knew she might not want me. But pathetically, I almost felt I needed her comfort as much as I wanted to offer her some. My heart burned when she leaned into me, falling against my chest, pressing her curly head to my heart. I wrapped her in my arms, thinking of all the ways she'd suffered. And all the ways I'd stop that from ever happening again. It wouldn't as long as I was around. If Von hadn't killed him, I would have. A new level of respect grew for the man.

"Are you sure?" she whispered. "Was he really going to—"

"Yes. And that's why you never heard from him again," Von told her. He looked agitated and paced the floor as she sobbed in my arms. Long minutes passed until her sobs faded into small gasps.

"Celeste—" Sunny began, and I knew he was dying to comfort her too.

"Thank you," she said, cutting him off. I turned to her in surprise. Von stopped his pacing and faced her as well.

"I mean, he wouldn't have succeeded of course. But if I would have had to face the attempt, the betrayal, not that it was unlike him. What could I expect from someone like that? What a jackass." She laughed, wiping away her tears that fell anew.

"But seriously, thank you for preventing me from having to do it myself," she bit out, as she used the back of her hands to wipe away more tumbling tears. Her voice was hard. It rarely was. But at times, when she wasn't a sweet, clumsy ray of sunshine like her father, she was hard as nails; Like that mother of hers that somehow was at the bottom of all of this.

"Yeah, well, you have shit taste in men," Von smirked.

"You've got me there," she smiled, the first genuine smile she'd had all night.

"I'm sorry I wasn't there," I told her, ashamed that Von was her protector when it was me that sat at her doorstep every night.

"Oh... it's okay." She pressed her small palm against my face and rubbed the skin there. I had dreamt of being touched in the flesh by her. Her daily pats to my stone form were teasing. But they didn't compare to this. I wanted this.

"Gargoyle, thank you for being there with me all those

years as my guardian, anyhow. That's what I always thought of you as. But I guess I had more than one guardian angel after all." She smiled and wiped away the last streams of wetness from her rosy cheeks.

She looked around the room, her eyes shimmering, as she pulled her hand away from me and bit her lip.

"Hey, guys...do you want to stay here with me tonight?"

I'm a slut, so shoot me.

After hearing what Von had done, the notes of love and regret in his voice had brought me to the edge of reason.

He had protected me when I couldn't do it myself. Sure, Mark was not the love of my life and I knew it, even then, but nothing stings quite as much as knowing that someone you might have loved was willing to kill you. I'd never been more mortified in my life to find that tidbit out. Nor had I felt such gratitude as I did to the three men who I knew instinctively would never hurt me that way.

As Von spoke, I saw it in all of their eyes: the misery in Von's, the warmth in Sunny's, the devotion in G's, and it pushed me towards a decision. I just couldn't stop myself using pesky logic anymore. Everything in me knew I was wrong. Giving them something like this was a taste of torture, wasn't it? Or was it just giving them a bit of what they'd wanted all along?

I didn't want to think of the moralities of it. I just wanted them to touch me and make it all make a little more sense before I faced tomorrow. The next step was to talk to my mother, who, for the life of her, would most likely do everything in her power to tear me down. I just wanted to be loved tonight.

"I'm going to take a shower. And then you all can too," I told them, running off to the bathroom where I cleaned up as best I could, given the tiny bottles of supplies the hotel came equipped with. I calculated out exactly one drop for each of the guys.

Refreshed, my clothes hand washed in the shower and set aside to dry, I pinched my dimpled cheeks and toweled off my curls. A little too excited, I walked out into the room, my body barely covered in nothing but a towel. I'd considered parading in naked, but I think they'd like to work for it right until the end, right?

"Who's next?" I told them, breaking them out of what appeared to be a lust filled stupor. I suppressed a giggle as their eyes popped open at my suggestion and they began to squabble over who would head to the bathroom first.

I thought they would begin a third bout of destruction if I didn't interject. "Sunny. You go," I directed, making the two hot-heads wait their turn.

In the interim, I talked to G some more. He was hot, yes. But I knew there was more to him, and I was determined to explore every inch.

"Want to sit down?" I offered as I sat on my bed, careful to cross my legs tightly. Didn't want to show too much just yet.

He had remained relatively quiet the entire time. Or was it that Von was just so loud that he left little space for anyone else? Either way, I wanted to hear more of him.

Despite how brutish he was when he first came into my house like he owned the place, he had remained so gentle and kind when it came to me. No matter that he was a tornado when it came to everything and everyone else. Despite admitting that I had no clue how to choose a man, I had to admit, there was something really attractive about his unpredictable nature. There was an awful lot that was attractive about the man, in fact. I knew facades were useless at this point, so with no demure eyes, no shy glances, I boldly slid my gaze over his face, taking in his stubbled chin, sharp jawline, and bright green eyes. My eyes drifted downwards, towards his solid chest that peeked out from his torn tee, down to his waistline, where his jeans hid what I was most curious to see. I had the decency to look away then. Though G made no move to stop me. He sat silently instead and stared me down, almost challenging me *to* look away.

Oh man, what woman didn't like the strong, silent type?

I cleared my throat and threw on a smile. "Can you tell me about gargoyles? I know there are many kinds of beasts, but I don't know the details. I should probably get to know you a bit."

"Nothing special about us. Not much to describe. My family, my kind, were cursed. Here I am."

"Nothing else to tell me? You could try convincing me of why I should be madly in love with you..." I joked.

If I didn't know any better, I'd think he had gone into shock at my words as he stared at me unblinking for a few minutes.

"Um," I began awkwardly. I hadn't meant to put anyone on the spot. It wasn't like this was a dating show. Though, that would be pretty cool, actually. It wasn't like I was successful in the dating game as of late. As a matter of fact, my dating life had taken a recent dive. If I didn't know any better, I'd think that was where the true curse lied. My eyes snapped to where Von sat watching us with sharp eyes. If I really didn't know any better, I'd think that one had something to do with my no-show dates over the last few months.

G's rich voice filled my ears, pulling my attention back to him with words that I supposed were meant to be romantic prose. An apparent answer to my earlier teasing question.

"I can fight. I can build. I can cook because I like to eat. And I am big."

"Shits sake," Von scoffed, rolling his eyes from where he sat on the little chair by the desk.

My lips trembled, tears springing to the corner of my eyes. I pushed my hands to my lips. *Hold it in...* I burst out laughing despite myself. And my dad said G couldn't make me laugh.

"Oh yes, you sure are huge." I drifted my gaze down his body once more. I was not a damn fool. If I was a human, I think a man of this size would split me in two. But given the circumstances, I was willing to try it out. A thrill of wonder ran through me. I begged the fates that he wouldn't let me down. Irony was sometimes the cruel joke that kept on giving.

"G, is everyone your size in your world?"

"No. Some are bigger."

"Shit," Von groaned, and I agreed with the sentiment.

"Oh, wow." Interest collapsed into fear. "Oh, no. You're not able to just come on over here whenever you want, right?" It was wrong to act afraid of him and his kind when he'd been nothing but nice to me. But I couldn't help imagining the great and terrible beings that might come barreling into this world. I racked my brain with tidbits of information about the other realms. I was pretty clueless about them, having only disinterestedly studied them as a kid. My knowledge pretty much concluded with the fact that the gods did whatever they wanted and were the most powerful beings in the universe. Who knew, or cared, what the others were up to?

"No, few can come here. And less can go back. I'm here to stay," he answered simply. I breathed a sigh of relief. I'd have to ask him more about his world later. Right then, a voice as radiant as a summer's day, interjected.

"In a way, I'm trapped here," Sunny said, emerging from the bathroom in nothing but a towel around his waist.

His words deserved a response, but all I could think about was how beautiful he was. His body was so fit and svelte, and a slight shadow of muscle outlined his smooth skin. His dark, wet hair framed his face like he was a painting, and those deep, silver eyes spoke ballads to me. I was enthralled. My core tightened in arousal and my skin burned with need. I squeezed my thighs together to keep from spreading them apart. I was so ready.

I watched as G disappeared into the bathroom while Sunny walked towards me.

He must have noticed that I was too absorbed in staring, to form words or questions because he continued.

"I came here by accident. I wanted to get back home at first. But I couldn't."

"You don't know how to get back?" I asked, mouth dry, as he came and sat beside me. I tried to focus. I did. But we were just one towel slip away from being naked on this bed.

I leaned towards him, hanging on his words.

"That's not entirely it. In truth, when I met you, I was captivated. I simply couldn't leave. That's it."

I blushed, watching as he looked at me, so soft, so sweet. My stomach tingled with warmth and my chest ached with longing.

"I'm going to kiss him," I told Von, hoping he wouldn't get jealous or feel awkward. Not waiting for him to answer, I leaned in and brought my mouth to Sunny's.

His mouth hung open a bit in what I guessed was surprise, as I moved slowly against him. I moaned between his lips. He tasted like peaches and open sky, and I urged him to give me more.

"Kiss back," I mumbled against his stilled lips. Obediently, he wrapped his arms around my shoulders and pushed himself into our kiss. His lips were soft, like silken pillows against mine.

I purred like a kitten and slid my tongue into his mouth. He shuddered, and it spurred me to go further.

I shifted, moving my legs so I could reach for his towel.

He placed his hand on top of mine, and I froze. His voice was a whisper, husky and slow. "I haven't done this before. I may not..." His voice shook, and I thrummed his lip with my thumb.

Guilt, in taking what I was not prepared to keep, and selfish joy that I'd be his first, battled in my chest. But I wanted him and knew he wanted me too. "It's okay. I'll be gentle." I smiled, kissing his chin and his jaw before coming back to his velvety, petal soft lips.

I slid my hand into the loosely fitted towel. I was surprised to find his dick already so wet, dripping pre-cum onto my hand as I moved to stroke him. He moaned into my mouth and I used the lubrication on my palm to smoothly rub him; a few soft, slow jerks, I timed with my kiss. He clung to my shoulders, and shuddered, as I felt hot streams of liquid coat my hands. I stroked him limp and kissed him softly as he placed his head in the crook of my neck, his breathing heavy and his moans gurgling in his throat.

It lasted only a few moments, but each stroke and

throaty moan I coaxed out of him was beautiful. Touching him, knowing how I made him feel, sent waves of pleasure through my body.

When he pulled back, his eyes were down-turned, his mouth trembled, and each breath was shallow. He looked miserable. "I'm so sorry. Was that—"

"It was perfect," I told him, taking my cum covered hand and bringing it to my lips. I licked at the flavor, savoring the salty taste. I smiled at the bashful bloom of color on his cheeks and kissed him again before I heard the bathroom door slam.

I jumped, remembering that I was not alone in the room, though no one had made a sound. Von was gone, and G stood in his place. His eyes wide and unmoving as he watched me wipe off my hands and cover Sunny back up with the fluffy white towel.

"My turn," G demanded. His voice was as unyielding as he was. But I liked the command.

A smile crept onto my face. There was either a magic wand or a huge dick standing at attention under his abysmally small towel, and I was more than happy to see what sort of magic we could get up to together.

"Sunny, do you want to leave?" I asked, suddenly aware how uncomfortable it might be for him to stay.

He shook his head. "I don't mind watching," he said, surprisingly easy going now.

I laughed. These perverted men...

"I know." I turned from him, allowing him to get comfortable in a seat across the room, while I beckoned Gargoyle my way.

"Can you be gentle?" I asked him.

"No."

"That works. But don't break the bed," I warned,

throwing my towel to the side and allowing them both to take in the curves of my body. I laid myself bare, unashamed that I was built like, well, a sex goddess with nice, round breasts and wide hips. I was curvy and not a bit apologetic about it. Being a goddess came with some perks.

After some moments of being eye-fucked, I smirked.

"Don't just stare." I laid back on the bed and propped my legs up, ready to receive him.

He stood for a second longer before he released the tiny towel that covered his jewels. And what a treasure they were.

"Oh my gods," I gasped at the sight of his erection. I'd had some encounters with penises that could give someone, well, a human, nightmares, but he blew away my expectations. G was perfect. The length was impressive on its own, but it was the girth that made my pussy quiver.

I gulped. I don't think I'd been this excited in my life.

He didn't speak, but the tiny glow in his eyes showed he was happy with my assessment. His next move took me by surprise when he fell on top of me, his large frame covering me entirely. He nuzzled against my face, running his jaw along mine, and I giggled as his beard tickled my delicate skin. His lips traveled down my neck, over my breast. I arched my back as he tongued the valley between my breasts, and with clumsy huge hands, squeezed them. I yelped and pushed myself further into his hands. He was rough, but it felt so good.

His wet tongue made paths all over my chest, creating a roadmap that outlined his brand of foreplay.

His hand slid down my body, and he stroked his dick a few good times. I barely had time to prepare myself before he plunged into me. "Oh, gods!" I screamed, covering my mouth with my hand to muffle my yells.

He wasn't much for taking it slow or prolonging the inevitable. A literal beast. He fucked me like he was ramming his dick into a wall. I mean, he must have assumed I couldn't break. Lucky thing for us both, that was true. I held onto his shoulders and let him ride me into oblivion. I loved the feeling of taking such a hard pounding that sent waves of pleasure to the tips of my toes. He consumed me. I'd never been with someone so large and strong, yet despite his earlier warning, he still managed to be a little soft with me. I kissed him hard as he ran one hand over my face, gentle and sweet.

With his other hand, he picked up my thigh, lifted my hips, and drove into me deeper.

I almost choked on my scream, but his big thumb landed at the corner of my mouth and I lapped at it, pulling the appendage between my teeth so I had something to hold on to as he continued to stroke me hard and deep.

"G, shit, G..." I said nonsensical words of pleasure as I fought to twist my body and rub my clit against him. I knew how to help us both get to where we needed to be. Bypassing the stamina that I was sure this beast of a man had, I rocked my hips and licked the shell of his ear. That finally earned me a tiny sound, almost a grunt, as he continued to push into me, even harder.

"Wait, wait, slow down," I advised, needing a little more time to build up my orgasm.

He did as I said, slowing down a bit, while I threw my head back and worked on pulling out our orgasms. Fucks sake, he was big. Just delicious. I gripped his shoulder hard, and ground down against him harder, fucking him back.

"Faster. Go faster now," I instructed him. He jack-hammered into me, and the bed creaked loudly in protest, almost gaining my concern. But that thought quickly dwindled as the heat of orgasm peaked and faded; almost there.

He was silent as he slid out of me and pulled back, hand on his cock as he spurted hot, white liquid all over my stomach. And right then, not a moment too soon, an orgasm of my own ripped through me, sending my toes out, and head back as I cried out his name. "Oh, my god! Fucking G!" I yelled, liking to hear my voice during the throes of passion.

More tired than he'd let on, he panted, harsh and rough, before he rolled to my side. We both laid on our backs, looking up at the ceiling, catching our breaths. My body was wet with his sweat and cum and I felt it slide down the side of my stomach with vague interest. I looked at him, our gaze meeting. His blonde locks were dark and clung to the sides of his face, and his vibrant eyes were alight with merriment.

"Too rough?" he asked.

"I'm still in one piece, aren't I?" I smiled back.

"But are you sure you've got energy for me now?" I heard Von's snarky voice interrupt. I sat up and looked his way, tossing some curls out of my eyes.

"Depends. What would you like to do with me, Von?" I goaded him. Part of me wondered if he was angry as he sat there watching me sex up G. I knew he was the jealous type, nor did he seem all that enamored with either of the other two men. But he just shook his head and smiled, dropping the towel to the floor. Full show of intricately tattooed abs and hard dick on display just for me.

"I'd like to do every goddamn thing to you."

Figurative horns sprouted on my head, accompanied by a devious smirk. "I like the sound of that."

Chapter Fourteen: Von

"Oh my gods, oh my gods!" she yelled, as she yanked a handful of my hair. I would have winced, might have pulled away if I wasn't so fully invested in eating the living shit out of her pussy.

She was sinful. I'd only been with one human woman, and so many dirty-ass demon women that I had lost count centuries ago. But this... this was divine.

She wrapped her legs around my neck, thrusting into my face for all she was worth, and I was more than happy to have her use me for her pleasure.

I moved my head wildly, rubbing my lips and tongue all over her pussy and clit, until she was practically levitating off the bed. She could have been. But again, I was just going along for the ride.

When she came, her juices thick on my tongue, I licked her clean. I loved the way she shuddered, crying out loud obscenities as she rode it through. Finally spent, she released my hair and relaxed her thighs.

I sat up, wiping her wetness from my chin.

I was so entranced by her. I loved her. Loved her to where I'd do anything for her. I had done more for her than she'd ever know. Like the other two, I was not supposed to be here amongst humans. It was not allowed unless, of course, there was no one there to stop you. The gods, for example, must have had the power to go wherever they wanted.

Not demons.

I was summoned to the human realm and I might have continued hunting, killing, if I hadn't laid eyes on her. When I found out what she was, I knew she would never have me. Not if she discovered what I was and what I'd done.

But nature is a bitch to fight against. Since the second I'd been able to interact with her, all I'd done was show her just what a murderous piece of shit I was. It was obvious I wasn't worth anything to someone like her, yet I still showed her who I really was.

Nevertheless, she wanted me. Wanted *me.*

With a gleam in her eyes, the temptress positioned us to her liking. She faced me, her eyes scanning my face and body with no shame in her lustful gaze as she threw her legs around my hips, almost like she was going to sit on my lap. Instead, she shifted closer and lined herself up with my cock. I shook the moment I slid into her slick pussy, a moan leaving me at how hot and wet she was.

Celeste moaned in kind, leaning back as she moved against me. I watched with hooded eyes as she moved her hips, leaned her head back, and called out my name. Her breasts swayed and bounced deliciously, and I wanted to lick her nipples and taste her again and again.

She leaned back further, propping herself on one arm as she slid one hand between our bodies, down to her clit.

With a loud moan, she began rubbing circles that were driving me crazy. I watched with glazed eyes as she kept moving against me. Our slapping flesh echoed obscenely in the poor human-occupied floor of this hotel, as she rubbed herself wanton and eager.

She smiled at me suddenly and sat up, pushing her fingers into my mouth. I didn't hesitate to take them in, licking her taste off of them, giving her satisfaction as she pulled her hand away and went back to rubbing herself.

"Shit, shit," she hissed before she fell back completely, and I adjusted, pushing my knees under her thighs so I could continue to pound into her. She was voracious, beautiful, and sensual. Her skin glowed with sweat. Her aura glowed with power.

Good thing she wasn't an angel, or she'd burn me alive.

I almost felt that way. That I'd die right then, buried eight inches deep in her pussy as the heat built and it shot out of me, an orgasm that reached from my balls to the tips of my toes.

I moaned her name, my dick and stomach muscles twitching, as I rode out the orgasm.

"Shit," I said, my brain clouded. My brow beaded with sweat. Instant anxiety hit me as I watched her finish herself off, her body convulsing, which caused my softening dick to slide out of her.

She moaned, and I watched with trepidation as she came down to earth. I had messed up. She didn't cum before I did. What the fuck.

"I'm sorry," she panted, surprising me. I should be the one apologizing for being a selfish bastard. "Poor timing. I should've let go a few minutes back, but it felt so good," she said, rolling over onto her stomach and stretching her back muscles. Her ass was pure perfection, and I wanted to lick her crack.

She sat up, eyeing me. “Are you okay?” She was beautiful. A ditz at times for sure, and a handful that rolled with weird-ass punches a little too much, but shit, I was with her finally. And I didn’t want to let her go. I wouldn’t.

“Yeah, you’re amazing,” I said.

She smiled and crawled over to me, pressing her mouth against mine and licking at my parted lips. I rubbed my tongue against hers, massaging the pink, wet temptation that licked and teased me.

“I’ll be back,” she moaned as she got up, running to the bathroom. I used my towel to wipe off my dick, half-assed as I laid back on the bed. I looked around the room at the two who had been all aboard for the impromptu train we just ran on the woman we were all madly in love with. Well, with Celeste gone, this was fucking awkward. I threw the sheet over my exposed dick and thought about her. Celeste.

Fuck. I still couldn’t get over the fact that I, a demon, was in love. But it was so easy to see why.

Celeste came back in after a few minutes, her old clothes back on. I smiled, ready to ask if she needed anything if there was anything else I could do for her. But she spoke first, saving me from the shame.

“Thank you, guys. I had a great night. But we should get to sleep. I have to rest up before I meet my mother tomorrow. We want this curse, or whatever it is, broken as soon as possible.”

She found the remote, turned on the television, and patted the bed beside her, inviting us into her bed when she had clearly closed us off from her heart.

My hands clenched, my heart dropping in disappointment and disbelief.

If I didn't love her, I would've ripped out her heart.

If I was going to see my mom, I needed new clothes and maybe a hairbrush. But I had no car and my purse was in the destroyed wreckage. Maybe it was already confiscated. If the police tracked me down as the owner of that mangled vehicle and went to my house, they would have most likely seen the destruction there. Then they'd check it out, find a shit load of dead bodies scattered throughout, and basically... I couldn't go back home because my life was over. I was on the run at this point.

I guess I'd be calling in some favors. Once all of this was over, that is.

I looked around at the three men who were all more or less off-putting today. G was pretty much the same, quiet and distant, but I could tell he was thinking something over in his mind. Sunny was looking a little anxious, and I wasn't sure if that was because of last night or the naughty things I had done to him this morning. He had lost his virginity in one more way at least—I licked my lips, remembering the way he had felt on my tongue. And Von, well, he was *off*. Arms crossed like a petulant child, he refused to speak to me most of the day. I ignored him as best as I could, but in truth, it hurt my feelings. I loved making love to him. He was amazing. And it had been more than just mindless sex for me. He had given me honesty, and protection, and kindness in a way I rarely received. Hell, he'd *killed* for me. So yes, it changed something for me. This let me know that Von, despite being, well, a demonic murderer, genuinely cared about me. My heart warmed to him, and the rest of them, and I was starting to almost regret letting them go. But there wasn't any other way, was there?

Nothing else to do but to solve this and end it, right?

Sunny bought me some new clothes, and then some lunch. The rest of the day was spent with them, simply wasting time. I needed to waste a shit ton of time before I could face my mom. I needed more time to steel my nerves against that woman.

But the more time I spent with those three, the more I knew wasting time was only going to make this harder. I didn't want that.

Another thing that was carrying on far too long was the attacks. I had woken up that morning hoping that the previous night's events had been a fluke. However, my morning walk was quickly interrupted by a sneaky little attack, followed by another. By midday, I was really tired of it.

I admit, I'd grown used to people thinking I was dumb over the years, so it didn't bother me much anymore, but the guys were annoying me with the way they purposefully thought they could keep me in the dark.

Sunny and Gargoyle disappeared sometime during my fifteenth trip into a clothing store.

It was not my fault that these places made clothes for twenty-one-year-olds who lacked half the assets I did. Good clothes were so hard to come by.

So I wondered at first if those two had just had enough shopping and simply left to do something else. I saw nothing out of the ordinary. At first.

But when Sunny and G had returned, roughed up, a guilty look on Sunny's face that seemed a permanent fixture, and a huff of angry aggression emanating off of G, I just had to say something.

"That's it. Let's go." I said, putting back the yet-to-be-purchased items and walking outside.

Once outside in the cool, sweet spring air, I turned an accusatory eye their way. My hands were pressed together as if I was praying to the gods for strength and patience. Which I was. "Another attack?" I asked.

They all shared a look that sent my hair standing straight up on the back of my neck.

"Don't do that. Don't keep some poorly concealed secret from me. Was it another attack with no explanation as to why?"

"Celeste, you're not in danger. I won't let you get hurt," Sunny told me, once again skating over the real issue.

I rolled my eyes at the way his sweet demeanor broke through my anger in an instant.

"Look, we should probably go now. It's getting late, and I'd rather not be here when they, whoever they are, come back." I looked around. We were a sight for sore eyes. Though we looked perfectly normal, more or less, our actions couldn't be so brazen and reckless in the daylight. If that little scuffle of theirs hurt humans, I wouldn't be able to forgive them, or myself, for it.

I inhaled deeply, enjoying the fresh air that just filled the lungs better than the recycled air inside.

The warm spring day was closing to a beautiful dusk, and I knew that my mother wouldn't answer if I waited past sunset. The little party animal let no one impede on her fun; her daughter, least of all.

I swung my shopping bags mindlessly as I found a spot outside of the shopping center that would give me a little privacy.

I sat on a little brick wall off to the side of a store, having no place else to go unless I was going to call for her in the ladies bathroom.

I focused as best I could, hating how my thin shorts did nothing to block the cool brick and hard feel of the material under my ass.

"I'm going to call for my mom," I mumbled to my three companions as my eyes slid closed.

"Mom. Mom... get your ass here," I muttered. Yet, unlike my dad's hasty answer, our connection lay dormant. I tried a few more minutes. Searching out a feel for other gods in the area. None. That mother of mine refused to answer.

"Motherfucker," I spit out, allowing my power to fade away into nothing.

"What happened?" G asked, coming to sit beside me.

"Exactly what it looked like. Nothing," I told him, running my hands through my hair. I was frustrated. It was almost dark. And if we didn't get in contact with her, I'd have no choice but to spend another night with them. I mean, I had a choice, but could I really control myself with these three?

"What to do? I need my mom to answer. The faster I get to her, the better."

"Why?" Von said, coming to stand in front of me. He had a pissed-off edge to his voice that put me on edge too.

"Why do you think? Nothing has changed. In fact, if anything, I realize I know nothing about any of you. Those attacks? These secrets? Why would I keep you by my side? I know next to nothing about you or this enemy. I'm just done with it. With all of this," I said, waving my hand around.

I cringed at my words and at the dejected looks that clouded their faces. I was sure Sunny was about to descend into tears. I closed my eyes. I was wrong for coming at them so harshly. But also, I had spoken nothing but the truth. I didn't know them.

"Then get to know us," Von said, head down as he looked at the pavement at his feet. His anger had seemed to evaporate in the wind. And so did mine. He had a good idea. Maybe there were more barriers to break down. Maybe I could give them a chance. I groaned. These men wanted to be with me, right? If I just got to know the men that had become invisible companions in my life, maybe that would be okay.

And even if it was just a curse making them feel like they wanted this... I cringed. I didn't want to think of that. I wanted to appreciate them and spend time with them, and worry about the details after.

"This might be totally messed up, but yes, let's do this." Three sets of eyes lit up like it was Christmas morning and I was the gift they were set to unwrap. I would not decline letting them do just that.

With growing arousal, spurred on by thoughts of our earlier activities, I knew where we had to go.

"Von, get us to a hotel." At least we hadn't been attacked there, for whatever reason.

"Here," he said eagerly, handing me a phone he slid out of his pocket.

"Whose phone—" I stopped myself from asking. I didn't want to know. The truth was, I was grateful for the little device. Life was so much harder without a cellphone.

I quickly called for an Uber to come and pick us up. I set the drop-off location to someplace near a hotel. Police tracking was something I had to be wary of. Gods, I'd turned into a seasoned criminal in the matter of a day.

"Well, they're on their way. We'll go to a hotel tonight and get to know each other." I flashed them a brilliant smile, despite knowing that this was wrong. Despite knowing that this was yet another way to avoid the inevitable. But it was easy to push those thoughts aside in favor of the easy way out. I always seemed to choose the easy way. "I'll give you a few days. So let's make the most of it."

Chapter Sixteen:
Von

We stepped into the warm afternoon sunlight, and I held in a cringe. Celeste had joked I was like a vampire with an aversion to sunlight. She wasn't far off base. "It's nice out today," she said. A dimple flashed cutely as she stretched out her back like a cat awakening from a nap.

"Eh," I replied. I'd hardly call a hot, muggy, polluted day in a noisy city, 'nice'.

"Why are you always angry?" Celeste pouted, pushing her pretty lips out in annoyance.

I stole a kiss, holding her against me, invading her mouth with my devilish tongue until I felt her knees go weak, her weight shifting into my arms. I abruptly pulled away, just to look into her glazed eyes; just to see her scowl in annoyance at me taking the upper hand.

I smiled at her irritation.

"I'm not always angry," I told her. I leaned against the hot iron railing of the balcony and looked out over our shitty view of the city. We were boxed in by three other buildings so we couldn't see anything except for brick walls and stacks of windows, yet Celeste insisted on coming out here for "fresh air". That was apparently a guise to hound me on my poor attitude.

"You are. You're always walking around like *this*." She made an exaggerated face, twisting her lips up as if she'd just bitten into a lemon, all while crossing her arms in faux intimidation.

I bit out an amused laugh.

"I do not look like that."

"Yes. You really do," she said, dropping her arms and twisted face to lean in closer to me. "And I don't understand why. I thought... well, I figured you'd be happy to be with me."

I held in a scoff. She had no clue. If she wasn't so beautiful and amusing, I'd hate her for her selfishness. But I'd figured out long ago that it was the nature of a god. Just like it was in my nature to harbor my fair share of dark emotions.

"If I'm angry, it's only because I am irritated by the questions that we still have no answers to. I don't know shit about those two," — I nodded my head back inside, where G and Sunny sat idly, talking about nature or some shit — "or my attraction to *you*. I'm angry that I've gotten myself into this. And that you have no way to stop it. My whole life, I've only known to fight when things didn't go my way. In my realm, it was either, be hard or get killed. Kindness is weakness."

"You can be kind when you're around me. I won't think it's a weakness. I won't hurt you."

"You really think that?"

She looked away from me, her gaze drifting down into the alleyway below that was littered with toppled over trash bins and wet pavement. "Was it normal where you come from to be this untrusting?"

"Yes. And it was also a given that I should have never fallen for you." She didn't speak, so I pushed instead. "Do you wish I hadn't?"

"I don't know." She was truthful at least, and I tried to think of that as a good thing. Better that than lashing out at her for making me feel stupid for caring.

In reality, I didn't mind being in love with this woman. If it had to be anyone, I could have fallen for much worse. Celeste was exactly my type.

Sexy and full of life. Sassy when she had to be, but not an overbearing bitch that had to pretend they were tougher than they were. She was strong, though. And that was something so fucking beautiful about her. The face of an angel, the power of a god, the body of a seductress, the clumsiness of a fucking cursed human. But she was mine. At least for now. I knew she was trying to use us. Get some dick and toss us to the side. She didn't have a mean bone in her body and didn't see it that way. But she had no intention of keeping us around. And I had no intention of letting her go.

Not since the day, I decided it was worth rearranging my entire life for her.

I WATCHED Paxus's black eyes gleam with malice. The sharp point of his chin and nose, and the thin splatter of greasy brown hair, made him look like a decrepit elf more than a semi-powerful demon. But I was under his command and listened closely to his instructions.

"Finally, a human has summoned me and I couldn't enjoy my time on Earth without my friends." He looked towards me and the three others who encircled him. "Friends" was a really strong word for people like us.

I had no fucking friends.

The only thing we had in common was the underhanded intention to use each other and anyone else we had to, to get stronger and join in the ranks of the Dark King's army.

Only the most powerful demons were recruited within the exclusive, elusive ranks of top demons, the ones so powerful they could wipe out worlds. Or so the legends went.

The only way to get that good was to be abysmally evil. And I was more than willing to try my hand at it.

"Yeah, well, what do you want us to do exactly? You were the only one summoned," I told him.

"But this human had enough hate and festering malice to open the portal for us all. Humans are so fun that way. Now come on, you three know what you're good at. Especially you Von. Put that killer instinct to work. You'll be rewarded if you do."

Indeed, this was my first time in the human world, and I had a dim excitement to finally get the chance to see what the hype was all about. Only demons powerful enough to grant humans desires were summoned, and only a summoned demon could walk in the land of man.

I walked off, uncaring for Paxus or the way he talked like he was on the brink of insanity. Though, to be fair, most demons were.

And I'd indulge in my fair share of chaos and madness before my time in this world was over.

As I WATCHED the girl bleed out, a skinny, homely little thing who couldn't have been older than her mid-twenties, I almost couldn't enjoy it. I felt little joy in the one thing I'd grown accustomed to doing so well. The fact was, this was not my victim of choice. This was a job, and there was nothing worse than turning a fun hobby into work. Truth be told, I was so tired of the shitty ass rules of my world. In the human realm, you could be evil of your own accord. It wasn't forced on you since birth. I had enough fucked up proclivities of my own without being summoned to murder for the simple fact that some lousy, sniveling human decided they needed supernatural assistance.

Weak.

They were so weak, and not to mention ugly, and they smelled rancid. Not that most lower-level demons in my world were winning any beauty contests.

"How many have you killed?" Kole asked me. He was a mousy demon who had recently been promoted to my rank of mid-level.

He still stank of lingering, filthy, wild darkness. I was seasoned enough in it. Born this rank, I didn't have to claw my way up from nothingness like he had. I had been a black-hearted son of bitch for over five hundred years.

"I don't know. Five? Ten? Does it matter? I'm just ready to get back home."

"You're right. But if I want to get stronger, I have to take advantage and kill as many humans as I can," he said before slinking off.

I sighed. I didn't give a shit what his life plans were. Demons were all out for the same thing. More power. And killing, hurting, was the only way to do it. Killing other demons assured the most absorption of dark energy, but humans worked too, if only providing smaller doses, making it more effective to kill more at once.

I was already bored by the third day of being there, however. Even killing wasn't fun when they were so weak they couldn't even put up a fight. At that point, I was fully un-entertained by these humans and all that they offered.

I screwed a cheap woman with lips the color of blood and the scent of unnatural flowers on her skin as I wasted time. I was not impressed and drank her blood, depositing her body behind the seedy hotel we had fucked in, just on the principle of her being a bad lay.

I sat on a random stoop in the city's downtown and took a long drag of a cigarette I stole off of someone's dead body. They wouldn't be needing them. I watched the people with lazy eyes as I drew my gaze up and down the street. Any second, I hoped, we'd be called back to our realm, having fulfilled our summoners' request.

Me and the others had helped him kill a myriad of blonde girls with blue eyes—probably the likeness of some girl that broke his heart. They held no charm for me. I was sick of seeing them squirm and cry when I took their lives. They weren't much fun. Human women never could be.

Then, I saw her.

Her blonde hair curled and bounced about her slender shoulders, instantly drawing me to her. She practically glowed in the dying sunlight. Unlike almost every other woman I'd seen, she was far from average. In fact, she was beautiful, in only the way the most powerful beings in my realm appeared. But she was no demon. There was always something cold about a demoness, no matter how pretty or how good it felt between her legs. But this woman surpassed anyone I'd ever laid eyes on. She looked warm and inviting, and my body ached from wanting her.

Suddenly, what should have been my prey had ensnared me.

Then she slipped on the stairs, tumbling down in a display so ridiculous, I almost decided against pursuing her, but I couldn't stay away. I took the chance to approach her, to say something that could get those pretty eyes to land on me.

But they didn't.

Sharp zaps of energy hit me in the chest the closer I got to her, but a little pain wasn't enough to dissuade me. Until it was, and I couldn't step closer without the power threatening to stop my fucking heart. Still, I was sure, as she gathered the last of the books from the ground, that she might take notice of me. And for a second, I thought she had. But I might as well have been invisible because she looked through me, past me, and then she was walking away. I trailed behind her, followed her to her little car, and when I went to open her door, I was once again painfully halted in my tracks. I couldn't touch her.

My heart swelled with frustration and confusion. She was somehow out of my reach.

Not *her*.

Not the first good thing I'd seen in this world, or even my own.

I stole a car and followed her down the winding roads to the suburbs a few minutes away, where she hummed her way into her home and closed the door behind her.

I walked around the perimeter of her little house, noticing the shifter planted on her front lawn, not doing shit. I would worry about him later.

All I knew was that the urge to go back home, to forget this mundane world and all the revolting people in it, dissipated the moment I saw her.

I was annoyed. Yes, angry.

Puzzled.

God damn horny.

And all I wanted to know was why the hell a being like that was living amongst humans and wrapping me around her finger so hard that I never wanted to let her go.

I'd never felt any angrier than the day I realized I had fallen for her at first sight.

SHE STOOD ON HER TIP-TOES, hands curling around my bicep, and planted a soft kiss on my mouth. I grasped the nape of her neck, tilting her head back and drawing her flush against my chest. A soft gasp escaped her, and I nibbled at her bottom lip before sliding inside, pulling moans from her sweet mouth. She murmured her pleasure, squirming against me as our tongues clashed in fervor, my left hand grabbing her by the ass and hoisting her against my hardening dick. I could take her, knowing she was ready for me to slide between her thighs. But I wanted to torture her; make her feel the same burning desperation I felt for her. Every day, and especially then, when I knew that kiss could be our last.

Anger, that too familiar feeling, stirred in my chest, and I tangled my fingers in her hair, took her bottom lip between my teeth, and bit down enough to draw blood. She flinched, and my heart raced, perverse satisfaction at hurting her, at tasting her blood, at claiming her, pushed me to punish her with my mouth until she trembled and moaned my name.

"Von," she quickly pulled away, gasping for breath, running her hands down my arms as she clutched onto my shirt, both of us painfully aware of my cock that was still pressed against her.

Her lips were swollen and red, blue eyes glassy, hair a tussled mess, and I'd never seen her more fucking beautiful.

She touched her fingers to her lips and sighed. "Let's go inside, Von." Desire colored her words as she slid the glass door open for us. If she wanted me to tell her more about my life, or my love for her, she never said. Instead, she paraded back inside, the scent of lust wafting off of her sexy body as she met the others in the living room.

"I really want to be touched right now." She cocked her head to the side and placed her finger under her chin in contemplation, eyeing all of us. "But I just can't choose. It would be so nice if you could give it to me in one go."

She was determined for us to take her all at once, but I hated sharing her as it was. I wasn't willing to compete with anyone while I was fucking inside of her. No, I wasn't done claiming her today.

"Only one Celeste. And I'm the one that got you nice and wet." I took her hand, my warning to the others, as I led her to the bed. I laid her down, towering over her supple form. "So let's make this easy. One's too big, one's too small, but one of us is just right," I told her as I pulled off my shirt. I knew she had a weakness for my tattooed abs. Especially the little new one in the middle of my chest with her name scrawled in blood red.

She laughed, throwing her head back at my words, before she crooked her finger my way, calling me to her. I didn't hesitate. Didn't need her to call for me twice. I'd follow this fucking temptress to the pits of hell... I knew she was the only one who could take me to heaven.

Tender lips on my face, on my neck, she explored my

body just as much as I did hers. Celeste made me lose my damn mind under her touch.

She was so beautiful under me, her huge tits pressed against my chest as I pushed into her slowly, savoring the throaty moan of pleasure she released as I took her. She liked to claw my back, pressing rounded nails into my warm flesh as she said my name, and I made her wriggle under me, desperate for release.

I teased her, drawing back from her, grabbing a pillow, and sliding it under her ass for a deeper angle. She whined, biting her knuckle as if she could suppress her cries. We both knew she wanted to fill up the room with her screams.

"Von, it's so good," she groaned, loud and unhindered.

"Do you like that, baby?" I teased her, slowing down so I could torture her with slow thrusts of my hips.

She bounced against me, trying to manipulate my pace. I had to be careful. She was too good at forcing me to lose my shit.

"Please Von, make me cum," she said in a breathless whine as she ground her hips in circles against me. I shivered and fisted the sheets by her head.

Fucking woman almost had me finishing at that.

I held her leg and angled in deep and hard. With one hand, I rubbed her clit and watched in rapture as she fell apart around my dick, her pussy clenching and soaking me, drawing out my orgasm.

I came inside of her, moaning her name. My arms shook, my stomach clenched, and having little strength left, I laid atop of her as she wrapped me in her arms. It would take a lifetime to get used to how intense it was with her. As I went to lie beside her, running my eyes over her smiling face, realism reminded me I didn't have a lifetime with her. I was only worth this fucking moment to her, and nothing beyond it. I ran a clawed finger over the curve of her cheek.

She really fucking thought that when we got answers, I would be done? She had no idea what I would do to stay with her. What I'd do to make her mine.

"When I was a girl, I never liked cake. Too sweet. But now I do." She looked at me expectantly.

I nodded, appreciating her nonsensical rambling even if I had nothing to contribute.

"I have grown to like a lot about this place. I barely remember Celora now. It's more like a distant dream." She rubbed her fingers up and down my arm as she looked off, her mind drifting to her memories of her long-abandoned home. I suppressed a shiver at her delicate touch, still not used to the feel of her on my flesh.

"Why don't you use your powers?" I asked. "Even against me. Like when we first met." I thought back to that night, not so long ago, when she could have struck me down. When her eyes seemed sharper than daggers and I imagined that if she had the ability, she might have blown me to shreds. Shouldn't a god have that sort of power?

She rolled onto her back and looked up at the white, dull ceiling.

"I don't want to. Didn't I tell you? Gods are greedy. Status hungry. If I had a taste of power, I'd want more. And how could I still be me if I became that?" She smiled, her dimples full—eyes shining. Tears there that she didn't shed. Wouldn't.

I wondered if she feared being a god. If one could fear something as divine as that, how could she stand me?

"Are you running from your mother?"

She sucked in a harsh breath. She released it slowly and closed her eyes.

"You're pretty perceptive." A smile crowned on her lips. "But everyone runs away from something, right?"

She shifted, facing her round, supple ass towards me, and scooted close. I held on. To her and the moment.

"But as I was saying, I think we need to stop by a bakery. You, never eating pie, is like a crime against humanity."

She babbled on about nothing, and I let her avoid answering me directly. I understood wanting to keep some things to yourself. So I just listened, nodding when I knew she expected it. Hummed in approval when necessary. I squeezed her, just to make sure she was there.

I didn't want to take it for granted, but it already felt natural to have her in my arms.

Celeste, my little woman, was finally snug in my arms. Her incessant talking eventually faded away to soft breathing. She wasn't asleep, just gazing at the bit of sky we could see above the buildings through the large glass windows. The sliver of moon in the sky indicated that it would be a new moon soon.

I didn't think about it often. I didn't think about the past. Just like Celeste said, there were things everyone ran from. But at the new moon, I couldn't stop myself from reliving the final moments that destroyed my world.

THE SOUND of cracking and splitting stone was the first thing we heard the day it happened. It hit us as only true fear could. Fear of the inevitable. Fear of death.

My stone fingers wouldn't flex. My hardened spine wouldn't help me stand. I fought with myself, urging my body to wake up, to fight and rip these creatures to shreds with my hands and teeth. But no matter what I did, it was impossible. *Helpless.* I was helpless to stop them.

Our enemies, the Anwa, were dangerous and vengeful creatures. They wore the head and torso of a human — Dubine, half shifters — and bore smirking mouths with venomous fangs. While their lower body crawled on eight shaggy legs, they outfitted each foot with a hard, nearly unbreakable jewel that made each powerful strike deadly. And like many in our realm, they hunted in packs.

They had found us. They had tracked us down into the dark caves at the unoccupied side of the east mountains and had discovered us poorly camouflaged among the stony grey stalagmite.

Crack.

I inwardly reeled from the ear-splitting sound. My ears burned at each strike they made against my kin. They taunted me with each clacking step they took against the hard stone ground. My hatred grew, my insides pooling with angry heat at the screeching burst of laughter that echoed against stone walls as they slaughtered.

I needed to move.

The attacks were closer.

Too close.

I had to rip them apart. I was stone, but I almost felt my

teeth baring, felt my claws elongating just enough to fight back.

Fight back.

The thought swallowed me. The idea of breaking out of my curse was so strong, I willed myself to materialize it into existence, even knowing it was impossible.

Fight.

I felt it then. A twitch of my hand, a shift in my center. It was no illusion.

I moved, my chest expanding with one deep breath.

Crack.

They were closer now, and the creeping clink of each step they took was a call to action.

My breathing sped up, my fingers clenched, my wings moved an inch, just an inch, and that inch meant everything, but it wasn't enough. The change was happening too slow.

Crack.

My sister was there, a few feet from me. My many cousins and brothers were there. Our family had seen its share of death. But together, we had managed to hide and survive as one of the last, strongest remaining packs of our kind.

But I knew I was losing them.

My sister with the big heart, who was beautifully larger than me and twice as kind. My brother, who challenged me daily with his hot head and biting words but also declared that he'd fight by my side for all our lives. My family.

Crack.

I extended my wings, the dark black and gray skin spreading out behind me, as I rose to my full height.

I was awake, the curse temporarily broken, and I snarled in fury. Fought in vengeance.

Gouged out the eyes of the creatures who looked at our sleeping forms and considered us easy targets.

I ripped out the hearts of the creatures who had taken my family, and security, and in no small way, my pride.

Blood dripped from my claws and fangs, and bodies lay strewn along the floors, but it wasn't enough.

Not when I saw her. My sister's half torn body was freshly changed into her soft flesh, but it was too late. She was torn apart, broken so that half her body was a bloodied puddle while the rest lay broken beside her. She twitched as if she sensed me, and I dropped beside her onto the cave floor that was a river of our blood, and their torn limbs.

"I'm sorry Tiab. I'm so sorry." But she didn't respond. Only stopped moving altogether, her body going lax, her eyes wide open and lifeless. Even if she had heard me, my words were as useless as I'd been. Useless to change anything. To stop them.

The bellow that left my throat was the last sound I'd make for a long while. Their names, the last words I'd say for years.

When I stumbled out of the caves and saw the sun rising, burning fury tore at my chest, this time directed at some unseen fate that played a hand in this tragedy.

Minutes.

They had found us out only minutes before sunrise. If only something had stalled them. Just ten more minutes and my pack would have had a fighting chance.

I stumbled through the forest, bleary-eyed and with a clouded mind. Unsure if I wanted to find the creature's home and exact my revenge, or if I wanted to wander off and calcify, never again to awaken.

After stumbling through the savage, dark terrain of my world, something pulled me deeper into the forest and I came out on the other side, somehow, in a world where I didn't belong.

⁂

"So I've told you all about Celora." In truth, she mostly talked about why she loved the human realm so much. "Now tell me about your home. Where do you come from?" She rolled over and rubbed her hands along the stubble of my chin.

"You know." I stroked the bare skin of her shoulder. I wondered if she'd read my mind. If she sensed the dark memories that were tumbling around in there.

She only grinned and shook her head. "No, I don't know. Not *exactly*. Tell me."

With the hand that was nestled on her hip, I held her tighter and drew her closer to my side.

I took a deep breath, unprepared to tell her of things that I found useless and trivial. It was all behind me. I had no past in a place where Celeste wasn't. I only cared about the future. But I humored her, choosing my words carefully as I began.

"The land is divided into hundreds of territories. Each beast takes and keeps that territory through battle. We are all territorial and have no issue shedding blood to keep what's ours." I rubbed the soft fabric of her dress and thought about what I'd do to protect what was mine. "But not all of us are equally blessed. Or cursed. There are those in the land that can shift into humans, like my people, those of Lansak. Others can never shift and they're the most dangerous of all. They can't be reasoned with. Can't be talked to. Not that we do much talking."

"Yeah, I've noticed you're pretty quiet most of the time. Any reason for that?"

My mind flashed back to the cave when words hurt more than they helped. I told her a half-truth instead. "I don't have much to say."

She rubbed her fingers against my hand. Her touch was light, cautious as she spoke. "I don't believe that. I think you have a lot to say. I bet you've been through a lot, too. You can open up to me. If you want."

I thought over her words. She wanted me to bare my soul and expose myself to her. I understood, even as she laid in my arms, that she was only physically available, but not really emotionally there. If telling her my secrets, some small part of them at least, might earn her trust and care, I'd try it.

"My people, the Bougles of Lansak lived in abandoned caves around the East mountain slopes and along the rocky coast. We never stayed in one place too long. We had the power to shift. But it quickly became a curse when two packs, the Anwa and Wovick, clashed with our kind. The Anwa were ruthless, but the Wovicks were even more dangerous, as they had found a way to use magic. I never saw it. But I'd heard of the battle my ancestors fought against them for centuries. To turn the tide, they cursed our kind. Ever since, we've been forced to shift on the new moon, unable to move, unable to fight, so they know exactly when they could come and slaughter us."

"What—?" she breathed out.

"They crushed us into pieces like cowards while we slept. We are conscious even while encased in stone. So each one of my kind felt every moment of their death. And when our size had dwindled down to near extinction, many of the last remaining families fled and hid out where they could. Mine included. Not that it helped." I exhaled a deep, steadying sigh. "I came here by accident. I stayed because I had nothing to go back to."

"I'm sorry. Not like sorry is enough. I don't really know what to say. It's—"

"You don't have to say anything. I learned long ago, words are not the only way to show comfort ... or even the best way."

She smirked and pecked my nose. "You hinting at something?"

"No hints." I grabbed her by the waist and rolled onto my back, placing her on top of my hardening cock.

I needed her to distract me. I needed to forget the underlying anger and violence that spurs those of my kind to vicious murder.

The one thing Celeste seemed to love more than talking, was sex. She rolled her hips, waking up my erection as her bare pussy slid against me. The woman didn't bother with modesty or undergarments, much to my pleasure. I pulled off her thin, floral blue dress, and loved the way her breasts bounced and swayed once free. I palmed them, squeezing hard.

She slid my dick out of my flannel pants and impaled herself in one smooth, practiced motion.

"G," she drew circles with her hips, and I held her waist so tight in my large, rough palms, I predicted bruising. "Thank you for opening up to me. I'm glad you're here." Her voice was a breathy whisper and I could almost feel some simmering emotion in the way she said my name that wasn't there before.

I growled low in my throat and lifted her before I slammed her down my length. She screamed out my name and using one of her legs as leverage she leaned both hands on my chest and took over the rough motions, slamming herself down over and over again until my body burned with the need to cum.

But Celeste had a cruel sense of humor sometimes, and I helplessly watched as she slid off of my still hard cock. A loud moan escaped her lips as she pushed herself up my body. She rubbed her tits against my chest, a teasing smile on her pink lips, before she pressed her mouth to mine. I didn't do kissing — still wasn't used to it. But I'd let that woman do whatever she wanted.

Celeste was going to do it, anyway.

She molded her breast in her hand before she pushed her hard nipple into my mouth. I sucked and licked while she stroked my cock long and slow. Her sounds of pleasure got louder, the rougher I was with her. I sucked her nipples between my teeth and bit lightly and she jerked her body. But she moaned from the pain.

She pulled away from me, popping her dusky nipple from my lips, and slid down my body.

I was fascinated at first until I understood what she was planning, as she went to wrap her lips around my erection.

"You don't have to—"

"If I can tackle it in the vagina, I can do some work with my mouth too." She smiled before she widened her jaw and pushed her pink lips over the tip.

It was so big compared to her little mouth. But she was focused, so greedy for my cum, that she moaned, mouth full of my throbbing cock, as she used one arm to balance herself, and her free hand to fondle my nuts.

I gritted my teeth.

Closed my eyes.

Felt her tongue swirling, lips working, hands moving from the base of my shaft to the head. Felt her little mouth right back on my dick, sucking me in. Pumping out my orgasm.

I grabbed the sheets so I wouldn't yank out a handful of curls.

My mouth hung open, a glaringly distorted look of pleasure on my face, most likely, but I couldn't control it. I couldn't control the way I jutted my hips, pushing my dick further into her mouth as I came, hard and hot. It felt so good; it fucking hurt. My chest heaved, breathing heavy and fast as she pulled away from me.

"Whoops," she said, and I looked at her smiling face through glassy eyes. "I made a mess."

I looked down to where cum and spit coated my inner thighs and softened erection.

She was not much for swallowing. I threw my head back onto the bed. I was one lucky son of a bitch either way.

Celeste laid across my chest, propping her chin up so she could meet my gaze.

"Are you happy G?"

I brushed a strand of golden hair from her cheek, imagining the golden-haired children we'd someday have.

"Yes. And Celeste, as long as I'm here, I'll protect you. You never have to change." I'd help her run away if that was what she wanted. As long as I was beside her.

Her eyes shined as she whispered, "I'll hold you to that."

Chapter Eighteen
Sunny

I walked out of the bathroom; the steam seeping like a mist into the wide open space of the hotel room. This room was, fortunately, bigger than the last few and had a separate living space where Celeste and the others lounged on the faux leather couches and watched a romance.

"Stop fighting over me! I won't choose. Not like this."

"It's him or me. But with me, you can be happy. He'll only bring you misery. You have to choose. And it should be me."

Celeste squealed, yelling out, "Don't do it! Choose the wolf, he's sexier!"

"Oh, now you think she should choose just one, huh?" I heard Von say as I walked towards the bed and dried off.

Celeste laughed. "Well, in the movie, she's going to do it, anyway. In real life... why choose?" she chuckled. I shook my head, still amused, if not embarrassed by her forward take on romance. I threw on my clothes, rubbing my towel over my dripping hair when I heard her footsteps shuffling along the carpet.

"Aww, dressed already?"

I turned, just in time to catch her in my arms. She pressed herself against me and pulled me into a deep, vanilla and cream flavored kiss. My insides twisted in love and yearning as she rubbed her tongue against mine, savoring me as much as she was begging me to taste of her. I moaned her name against her lips, wrapping my arms around her waist, desperate to mold her to me. My whole body sizzled when she touched me. She was my life source in those moments, physically affecting me to the point where I felt the electricity of her kiss was the one thing keeping my heart beating. And I further broke, knowing I needed her more than what was rational. I was desperate for her. And that very need caused me to become the person I'd dreaded.

With a final lick to my lips, she pulled away from me. "I missed you," she sighed against my cheek and I held her close as she breathed me in. "You smell so good, Sunny."

I laughed. "Hotel shampoo and body wash."

"No, it's you. I refuse to believe otherwise." She pulled back and ran her eyes over my face before they landed on the jewel in my ear. My heart fluttered painfully.

"Hey, did you shower with that? I don't think I've ever seen you take it off."

I pulled away from her. My hands shook as I fingered the stone gently. "Yeah, it's precious to me."

"It's really pretty. An emerald? I've never seen anything that color green before. Can I—" She went to touch it, and I grabbed her wrist, so fast, it startled us both.

I let her go, shame and fear burning my insides as

though a stream of molten misery was flowing inside of me. "Please, don't touch it."

"Sorry. I didn't mean to upset you." Her eyes were wide with doubt and undue guilt.

"No, you didn't upset me." I pulled her back into an embrace. But she was tense and rigid in my arms. I hated myself for that. "I'm so sorry, Celeste. It's the only thing I have from my realm. I need this. It's important." I pressed my lips together, afraid I might spill my secrets to her then. I knew she wanted to know more about me. About my past. I'd told her just enough to keep her distracted from those questions that would reveal all of my faults, and all the reasons she should hate me. I'd never told her about the stone, and why its presence here meant that she and I were fugitives. I couldn't tell her that. Because then I'd have to admit that my selfishness, my want for her, had been the sole reason she had to uproot her very life.

"I understand. I have something from my realm too." Her eyes lit up as she described a little porcelain doll she had back home that she planned on passing down to her daughter someday. "It's one of the most precious things I own."

"You're the most precious thing to me, Celeste. Not even this stone compares." I kissed her temple and her soft cheek, and she greedily brought her lips to mine.

I melted in her kiss, putty in her hands as she roamed free across the plains of my skin, the curve of my tongue, her hands a rake in my hair, husky moans a song of her lust.

We backed up to the bed, and I sat heavily with her straddling my lap. I'd tasted her kisses and felt her hands on me so many times, but this time, the tension was thick in the air, and my desire for her was too much to placate any other way than to make her mine completely.

She ground against my aching erection. The material of my pajama pants was so thin, I could feel the heat of her core through the fabric and I shuddered, sliding my hands under her shirt, and palming her heavy breasts until she moaned, encouraging me to go further. I pulled away from her mouth, lifting her top and swirling my tongue over her pebbled nipples. She grabbed ahold of my shoulder, grinding against me while pushing her nipple further into my mouth. I sucked hard, rolled them gently between my teeth, and was rewarded by a sweet gasp as she grabbed a hold of my hair. Had it been just one week back, I knew I would have already climaxed by that point. But right then, I wanted so badly to be inside of her. To feel her wrapped around me at last. I pulled away from her chest, still molding her breast with my hand as I brought my lips back to hers.

"Celeste, can I—"

"Finally going to get your dick wet?" Von sneered from the entryway with G at his back. I pulled away from her swollen lips, and tried to ignore the antagonizing note in his voice. I imagined he was battling his own displeasure at having to share her. I hid my face in the crook of Celeste's neck, placing a soft kiss there; under the cover of her curls and the guise of shyness, I could easily hide my smug smile at the demon's apparent discomfort.

"Give us some space, guys. Have some decency," Celeste reprimanded, shooing them away from where they stood, apparently prepared to watch my "deflowering" as Von had tauntingly put it.

I could almost feel his eyes boring into me as he said, "Be easy on him, Celeste, and I'll be right here if he can't satisfy you, sweetheart."

They shuffled back into the other room, which was just

one short hall away. I almost regretted their leaving. I didn't want anyone to question the fact that she desired me and claimed me just as much as she had the others.

But his words did hit me right in my confidence, and I felt the tightening in my chest increase and the ache in the back of my skull from wound-up nerves begin to pound.

I couldn't admit my fear to her. Masculine pride and desperation to please her battled for dominance within me. And just when I thought the decision to act bravely, even seductively, had won, my hands trembled, my breath hitched in my throat, the moment she ran her fingers through my hair.

"Are you ready?" she asked, placing a breathless kiss to the corner of my lips, and grazing her soft hand over my cheek. She started moving her hips again, bouncing and twirling circles against me, and I bucked my hips against her core, near desperate to have her.

I nodded. Doubts began to fade as Celeste worked her body over mine, and heated desire rose to the surface of my skin.

"Don't worry. You won't hurt me. And I won't hurt you," she said, a whisper in my ear as she licked at my earlobe, sending a bolt of pleasure through me.

I nodded again, unable to speak at the love that filled my heart. The tremor of nervousness and desire that coursed through me took the words out of my mouth. She had already teased me, taught me so many ways to physically love her with my mouth and hands. She was my teacher, and I was eager to learn every single means to please her under her thorough tutelage. I was intoxicated with love and somehow it was enough to dissipate some of the fear that threatened to ruin this moment. It was enough to spur me to kiss her without her encouragement, to wrap my arms around her slender shoulders and reposition us so I could push her backwards into the wrinkled sheets and plush mattress.

She was tender and seductive, a gleam in her eyes as she undid my shirt, pulling it over my head before she pulled the straps of her top down, while I hiked the hem up. She forced me to love her, equal parts sweet and hard. With her hands in my hair and her tongue sliding against my lips, she soothed my worries. I trusted her with everything I had. Trusted her with my body, because she'd be my first, and my last. Gladly, I gave her my heart, knowing she might not want it.

I didn't take my eyes off of her dazzling blues while I slid into her sweet wet flower inch by inch. I moaned, deep and loud, overwhelmed by the heat of her around me as she sucked me in. I had to release her gaze then, dropping my head to her shoulder to release a shuddered breath.

She wrapped her legs around my waist and moved against me. I stilled, my body straining to maintain control. I remembered what she taught me, and I tried hard not to release too soon, but this was different. Much different from her mouth and hands.

"It's okay," she whispered against my ear, using her legs to draw me in deeper. "You've got it."

Shivers ran down my spine. I didn't want to disappoint her. I wouldn't tonight.

I finally moved, allowing my hips to propel shallow thrusts into her core. It was so natural. Making love. Doing this with Celeste. The only one I'd want to have me this way. I rocked against her, and she moaned my name, her warm breath against my skin, causing another bout of shivers to run down my spine. I watched her face, looking at every fine detail as I was connected with her this way. In her arms. Inside of her.

"Move faster, Sunny. It will feel better for us both if you do."

I flushed, and picked up the pace, hiding my face in the crook of her neck as I pushed against her. I groaned at the hot, wetness that coated me, and the feel of her soft breasts against my chest. Soft gasps and low mewls tumbled from her soft lips as she wrapped her arms around my shoulders.

"That's it. Harder, Sunny." I gripped the sheets, pulled my knees up so I could angle in deeper, slowing down my pace to pull out and slide back in with a sharp thrust. I flushed at the sound of our bodies slapping together. She groaned and wriggled beneath me, trailing her fingers down my back, and up the column of my neck, where her fingers tangled in my hair. "That's it, fuck me, baby."

I clenched my teeth, grunting in searing pleasure as I felt my orgasm build. The heady need to speed up and reach an end almost overtook my logic. I pounded into her, new desperation filling me as I came undone against her, letting my lips trail her soft skin, leaving sloppy kisses and languid licks along her lips and neck. I finally gave myself to her as I moved my hips with more fervor. I was pushing into her with a frantic pace that I was helpless to control. She clung to me harder.

"Yes, yes, does that feel good?" she whispered, placing a wet kiss on my lips.

My stomach rolled, goosebumps spreading over my skin. "Yes, it feels so good inside of you."

"Sunny, baby, sit up," she said, pushing me off a little while she continued to move her hips against me. "Look at this," she breathed, her eyes traveling down my body to the place where our bodies were connected.

My skin burned as I watched myself move in and out of her.

It was indecent and the most erotic thing I had yet imagined as I thrust in and out of her folds. She was beautiful. Every inch of her.

She put her leg on my shoulder, and I shuddered as I felt her finger trail down my chest.

"You're so good, Sunny. It feels so good." She squeaked suddenly, and I saw her body tense as she fell into an orgasm.

I stopped. Unsure what I should do.

"God, no Sunny. Keep going," she groaned, and I nodded, leaning back into her so I could kiss her lips. I loved her kisses, how soft and loving they felt. I wondered, hurting myself with the thought if she could learn to care for me someday.

"I love you, Celeste. I promise I'll love you for all of my life." My vow to her, the one I'd held inside of my heart since I first laid eyes on her, slipped past my lips before I could stop myself.

She blinked at me, then nodded. She turned her face from me, hiding against my shoulder, and I continued making love to her. I pretended I could be content with just this moment. I could pretend not to have seen the fear burning in her eyes.

It was difficult to tell the difference between the first time I knew I was in love versus the first time I was willing to admit just what that would mean. I wasn't even fazed by how little time had passed, being that I was soft-hearted and the kind of girl that wore her heart on her sleeve. And these men went straight for the heart.

I looked around the small living area, pressing deeper into G's side, shifting my leg over Sunny's lap, while I ran my hands through Von's tousled hair as he sat on the floor, his back pressed to the couch.

I scanned the room once, twice more, memorizing it because I knew, like we all did, that something like this might not last. *Wouldn't* last. But gods, the thought threatened to break me.

When they touched me, when their lips pressed against mine, when our eyes met, I knew it was more than just lust I felt for them. It was easy to admit that the way I melted when they smiled at me, said sweet words to me, hell, even fought me, was my first clue. They made my insides blaze with longing and desire, apprehension and excitement. They made me feel found when I'd thought for a long time that my true self was never good enough for anyone. They saw my faults and wanted me despite them. I knew in my soul I could be happy with these men for the rest of my life.

I had found a sparring partner in Von, who would talk insane levels of crap just to rile me up, but use that same delicious mouth to kiss me senseless. And yes, the man was unreadable at times and stewed in his anger often. I didn't like that shit because I wasn't a negative person. Even with my life in the trash bin, and death seemingly chasing us at every turn, I didn't let that get me down. But it got to Von. He only saw the negative, and I guess that made me have to shine extra bright to make up for it. I was goofy and seductive with him. I tried to get him to laugh and sometimes succeeded. I learned he liked action movies and burgers. He liked dirty talk and watching me play with myself. He had taken to calling me his little temptress, and I tried to turn that on its head when I'd break out the jokes just to see him break that cold exterior and smile.

Sunny would nearly radiate with his tenderness and care for me, taking any opportunity I gave him to gaze deep into my eyes until I was sure he memorized every speckle of blue in my irises. There was nothing more precious than the way he sat hugging a pillow while we watched television dramas together. And the tears in his eyes when he'd see someone proclaim their undying love. He was so sensitive. But even when Von tried to best him, he never submitted. As a matter of fact, there was something about him that seemed hidden beneath that sweet face of his; something that simmered like hidden strength and a touch of darkness, and I loved it. I wanted to delve deeper into just what made him so gentle with me, but so calculating at times, as if he knew just how cruel the world could be and he was prepared for the shit bomb that could drop any second.

I adored G and the way he was far more easy going than I first took him as. Yes, sometimes he clammed up and just sat back and observed. But there were also times when he was nothing but a sweet teddy bear that washed my hair in the bathtub, broke into bakeries at night and brought me back sweets, learned how to play a mean game of Uno, and drank liquor like his stomach was steel lined. More than that, he made me want to actually envision a future unlike any I'd had before. One where I was safe in his arms, his heart beating against me, while nothing else in the world mattered more than just existing for one another. We didn't talk about his past much, but he painted me portraits of what he saw for his future. *Our* future. He made it so simple. *Just exist, and I'll do the rest.*

Yes, loving them was too fucking easy. And to be honest, it came as no surprise because I knew from day one, these were the kind of men that would be my undoing.

I said from the beginning that I did dumb crap when it came to men.

But this was maybe the worst thing I could have ever done. I didn't think I had steered them, or myself, too far off course, even knowing I had let myself fall in love with them. Until last night.

When Sunny had proclaimed his love for me, my initial elation plummeted into festering guilt. I knew he loved me, and I had selfishly taken advantage of that. I practically begged for his heart, his body, when I knew better than anyone that there was a very real possibility he didn't actually want me. My stomach rolled with the implications of what I'd done. What I'd taken when I didn't deserve it.

But I loved him. I loved them all. And as much as I wanted to run and hide from the origins of our relationship, I couldn't. Running was not possible this time.

I just couldn't ignore the fact that some divine intervention had, without doubt, brought them to me. In believing that, I had to accept, too, that they weren't really mine.

Back and forth, I let myself ache and hurt over it. Over what was right and wrong.

Was it wrong for them to just want to be with me? They knew me inside and out. And despite knowing they carried around dark secrets from their pasts, I still felt like I had learned an awful lot about them.

I was so in love my stomach fluttered with a million electric butterflies, when I so much as thought about them. Something as beautiful as that shouldn't have to be hampered by guilt and pain. I didn't know what to do about it. It was breaking me.

I clicked off the television, my mind way too full to pretend that I was focused on the movie I'd already seen a dozen times. Dude sinks to the bottom of the Atlantic. *Three cheers for happy endings.*

"I was watching that," Von groused, before he reached over and tried to snatch the remote from my hand.

"Come on, I'm hungry. Let's go out for an early dinner," I said, standing to my feet and sliding into my flip-flops. I needed some fresh air. After endless days of evading some unseen enemy, moving hotel to hotel, and spending most of my time having a ton of sex and learning just why these men deserved my heart, I wanted to get out. I needed to clear my head, and I hoped that clarity would end with a decision.

"HELLO, Sunshine Hearts Preschool. How can I help you?"

My boss's voice grated at my ear, but I was cordial when I had to be.

"Hello, this is Celeste."

I blinked, counting the moments of silence. I wondered if she hung up at the sound of my voice.

"Celeste doesn't work here anymore," she said after a while, and I sighed, sadness and anger battling in my mind. I mean, I knew it was coming, but who enjoyed being fired?

"I'm really sorry for disappearing on you, but I was in an accident and some things have happened—"

"Another accident. Another bumper-to-bumper because you were daydreaming? Another coffee spill or slip on a slick floor? Honestly, I don't have time for this. I was going to let you go nicely. Even offer for you to finish out the month for one last paycheck. I am sure you could use the money. But this is inexcusable. It's just best you come get the rest of your things and—"

"I won't be back. My car was totaled. My home was destroyed. I have no money, and I'm barely making it right now. But you know what, I'd rather be half-dead laying in the streets than deal with your vindictive, holier-than-thou bullshit anymore. I sort of thought people had to just deal with bullshit bosses like you. But I realize, you're just a fucking asshole and that isn't something I have to put up with anymore. Tell my babies, Ms. Celeste misses them. Thanks a lot. Have a nice day, you evil bitch."

I hung up so fast; I was sure I had tapped into godspeed to accomplish the feat.

My fingers shook with adrenaline, and my face burned with embarrassment and shame. Sure, I was wrong for not finding the time to call into work. And yes, I deserved to be fired after disappearing for a week. But I sort of had other issues to deal with. Not least of all was the fact that anywhere I went, an attack was sure to follow. I wouldn't have dared bring that back to the center and possibly bring harm to the children. *The children.*

My heart sank, and for the first time since all of this began, despite losing my house, car, and job, I realized this was the one thing I was most heartbroken to have lost. I let out a watery sigh and squeezed my eyes shut, swallowing down the tears that I refused to spill.

This was the final straw. One of the final sentries, I had erected to stave off my place among the gods, had so easily been toppled. *Shit.*

I groaned, taking heavy steps back towards my table. This was really just the natural progression of how all of this was going to end anyhow. Even if I were human, I was still going to end up jobless and telling my boss off someday. I really told her off. My lips twitched despite the heaviness in my chest. I took in a deep breath, and my mouth curled into a small smirk at what I'd just done. Granted, that wasn't how I planned my call to go, but I did think it came out pretty good. I mean, I cursed her out a little at the end there, but overall, I stayed professional, cool, calm and collected. I chuckled to myself, knowing I was full of crap and with a breath that felt like relief, I smiled up into the grayish-blue sky. *Yeah, I let my job go. I let one more piece of my mask slip.*

Head held high, I walked over to my group.

"Did you do it?" G asked, throwing me a questioning gaze as if I'd back out.

"Ha! Of course I did," I said, snatching a fry from Von's bag.

"You told the bitch to drop dead?" Von said as he leaned back in his chair, legs crossed at the ankles, while he took a sip from his soda cup.

I sat down heavily on the wobbly metal chair, grabbing my half-eaten burger.

A sudden burst of nerves had caused me to stop eating mid-chew just to get the deed over with. Though she technically fired me before I had the chance to quit, the results were the same in the end.

"No, I didn't tell her to drop dead, but I called her an evil bitch. I'm so wrong for that." I smiled, chewing my food and snatching up another fry. "By the way, on the note of evil, are all demons evil? I never met one before you."

"Yes. All of us," he said, sitting up and putting his drink down. "The truth is, the more powerful we are, the more evil and twisted."

"So, is there really a King of Hell?" I whispered. There was a lot about the different worlds I didn't know about. I found it all sort of boring when I was younger. I wasn't much for travel, studying, or, well, learning. I did my time in high school and college. That was more than enough for me.

Von looked off into the sky as if considering my words and how much he should reveal. "Yes. But it's not what you think. And I'd never met him myself. Only heard rumors. Only the most powerful, or most unlucky, meet the Demon King. Even someone like me could fear someone like that."

I mulled over that, chewing on a fry with just as much contemplation. I didn't want to pry, but I wondered for the first time just how bad Von was, and if he'd done things, I wouldn't be able to forgive.

I pushed the thought aside. In the end, it was his business, and I didn't need to deal with yet another complication in our relationship.

"Well, I'm glad you're here. You don't have to live with that kind of stress."

"Things are tough here too, Celeste. I think you know that," Von answered.

I looked off into the distance, over the half empty parking lot in a little city that had more human suffering than I ever let myself take note of. I may have had magical abilities, but I was no hero. Just wore the human costume but had no intention of peeling that off, throwing on a cape and jumping into action on anyone's behalf. Yeah, like every other god, I was a selfish bitch.

Suddenly, not so hungry anymore, I rubbed my palms together, tapping off the invisible crumbs there, before I pushed off the table and stood.

"Okay, we should get going," I said.

"Wait," Sunny said, his face tense, lips tight. "Let's go this way." He stood and began walking away without another word.

"I was going to have an Uber pick us up if—" I began.

"No Uber, Celeste. Just follow me. Please," he said, a tight, soft smile on his lips.

I nodded, walking after him, trying to keep the pace. I knew that look. My stomach dropped in annoyance and worry. Sunny always sensed them first.

"Sunny, slow down." His steps were almost frantic, urging us to almost break out into a full run at his heels. He'd never reacted so fervently before.

He stopped momentarily and grabbed my hand, pulling me along.

"I can't. I wish I could, but they're—"

Something stung me, a piercing pain in my shoulder that burned and tingled along my skin. Sunny's words slipped into background noise as the world muffled around me. A feeling of sudden drowsiness overtook me and my head spun, aching and turning all at once.

I stumbled on my feet, and I felt a sickening drop in my stomach before Sunny caught me in his arms.

"Celeste..." he began and mumbled words in a foreign language that I couldn't understand. I didn't need to understand his words, because I felt the panic and fear in his shaking hands and in his pleading voice. Von and G called my name and for a moment, the world was in slow motion as I watched Sunny's face fade behind my slowly closing eyelids.

My body had caught fire under the afternoon sun, and I was falling into stifling black, in the arms of someone who whispered in my ear, deep voice rumbling like rocks around me. Soon, I was gone.

Chapter Twenty: Sunny

My body shook. Every nerve felt raw with pain. Her name bubbled to my lips. *Celeste.*

"Celeste!" I called out, my voice cracked, my legs were weak, unable to hold me up any longer. I was weak. More so than I'd ever been in my life. Too weak to help her now.

"Tell me what's going on!" Von shouted at me, shoving me hard as if to bring me back to my senses.

It helped. I blinked and looked around at the encroaching threat. But there was no time to run like I had planned. No time to get us out of this, or save Celeste. Not then, when the area was suddenly covered in shimmering green energy that colored the world a distorted landscape of verdant and warning.

They had finally come for me with all of their forces. I had evaded them for so long. But I knew, I knew all along this day would come.

I looked at Celeste, my very soul, lying incapacitated in

G's arms.

She was ethereal even then, perfect and vulnerable and hurt. And it was my fault.

I should have left her when I had the chance.

I should have left.

"Is she alive?" I whispered, and my voice didn't even sound like my own anymore. It was too frail and choked, like an old man fighting to say his last words.

"Yes," G replied, his unwavering voice comforting me. For her life, at least, I was thankful; and for his strength.

Determined to end this, no matter the cost, I called on my power, feeling the surge of energy come to my hand and so too did I demand a long-dead part of myself to resurrect so that I might win this battle for Celeste's sake.

Strength back in my voice, sturdiness back in my limbs, I warned my comrades, "We are fighting against the dark queen's guard. Please be vigilant. They are among the most powerful in my kingdom."

"So, they are from your realm. And you seem pretty fucking familiar with them," Von grit out, backing up so that his back pressed against mine. "I knew this involved you. But god, if I have to fight a bunch of fairies, I'm not sure I can live with myself. No matter how powerful you claim they are."

I didn't answer. He would see soon enough. I was surprised that he couldn't feel it for himself. The amount of dark energy that spread like a cloud of poisonous gas around us was enough to make it difficult to breathe. I knew that was exactly what they had intended. They were here for my life.

They would not have brought out this much power if their intention had been anything civil. We were long past negotiation. They had found me, and it was my folly for staying in one place so long. In the past few decades, since my descent into this world, I had drifted from place to place but always returned here to see Celeste. I knew better back then and never stayed more than a few days at a time. But in wanting her, having her, I ruined it for us both.

My power swelled within my hands like molten lava. I didn't have time for regret. I had within me the ability to do what I'd always done; fight. I held my arms up towards the unseen enemy and liquid silver streamed out in every direction.

Just the threat of my touch should have been enough to make them think twice before an attack. But these soldiers were brazen, sending out energy blasts and poisoned spears towards us with more frequency.

If I didn't know any better, I'd think these soldiers didn't know who or what I was. If I didn't know it made no sense at all, I'd have thought that they were trying to incite my rage.

Spears of energy flew past Von and me, and we dodged and dove out of their path. These soldiers liked to play in the shadows. Staying unseen was their primary tactic and their only saving grace. Magic was a long-distance move they utilized well. But so did I.

I felt my power slither like a silvery snake along the pavement, into the misty shadows. As if having a life of its own, it grabbed greedily onto unprepared soldiers and swiftly took their lives.

I looked to G, hoping he was protecting Celeste from further attacks. He was rather impenetrable. His skin had turned to cold stone as he held on to her body, and a few stray attacks grazed off of his flesh, causing no harm. At least she was safe. I needed to make sure she stayed that way.

"Get Celeste and leave. I will handle this," I told Von, preparing for the counterattack.

Von scoffed, "Like hell, I'm leaving. Let them come out so I can rip them apart."

"You may be a demon, but their powers are superior to yours. Don't be foolish."

"You have no idea what I'm capable of," Von hissed. And his power took form, a dark mist of energy that spread out alongside my own.

"You have no idea what they're capable of," I shot back as I dodged another attack that nearly impaled me right between the eyes.

Our fights thus far had been against weak creatures. Scouts who only sought to gain knowledge of my whereabouts and subdue me with the intent to capture. I knew the queen. She wanted me back alive and most likely returned to her captivity. I would die before I allowed it.

"Oh, goddess," I heard behind me. "I think the question is, does anyone have a single clue what *I'm* capable of?" I turned to find Celeste was on her feet, walking towards us, a ray of power and light creating a shimmer all along her skin. Stars were in her hair, sunshine in her eyes. She was pissed.

"Who are these people?" she demanded, and I didn't have the strength to deny her this information anymore.

"They're from my realm. They... they're..."

"They're after Sunny. And you got pulled into this because of him," G said, coming from behind her.

"No shit," she whispered. Within moments, she had unleashed a layer of power, like a blanket of white light that fell over the area. It fell like a dazzling net around us, and she held the strings. I gaped in amazement and apprehension. I'd never seen her so fierce.

With a yank, she tumbled forth a dozen dark soldiers that were now ensnared in her hold. That was even more than I had assumed was on the attack.

These were indeed elite soldiers, so in that regard, I had been correct. Uniforms of dark green covered their bodies. Dark vines intertwined in the design, and deep wooden brown made up their shields and armor. They were a mockery of the beings of light that lived in our world. And they differed from them in another distinct way. Darkness leaked from their black eyes, spreading like poison on their skin. These creatures pulled their power from darkness, and when in battle, they *were* darkness.

But even as I calculated their next move, their power, I realized too late that I was glorifying them and underestimating Celeste.

"You, Fae, explain why you just poisoned me? Or why you wrecked my car. And helped finish off my house? And have been chasing me for like, two weeks now!" Her voice rose in intensity, her anger now at its pinnacle.

Bound, they struggled, ignoring her words, calling out blasphemies that they were fortunate she did not understand. I tensed, still afraid that they'd somehow gain their freedom.

She pulled the net of energy again, and the soldier grunted in pain. "Answer me..." she beckoned, and I felt my head spin at her words. I blinked away my sudden vertigo and turned to the leader who leered at me as he said, "We are after him."

"Why?" Celeste demanded.

"He is a thief. That filth has stolen a most precious relic and even if he returns it, that would not be justice. He pays for this crime with his life," he sneered.

Celeste turned to me, her large, soft eyes full of questions and confusion.

"Sunny, is that true?"

"Celeste," I whispered her name, a plea, a prayer for her

to accept what I was going to admit. I couldn't hide behind lies anymore. "I stole, yes. They are right to seek me out."

I turned from her before I could see any disappointment in her gaze. No longer did I have it in me to keep running for my life. No longer did I care about my original quest, or why I had done the things I had done. But I cared in desperation what she thought.

"You can hand me over to them. I deserve punishment, I know. But I couldn't turn myself in until I got to meet you. Until I could touch you, Celeste. When I came here, it was to hide. But I stayed because I needed you to see me, just once. And now you have. And more than that, I've kissed your lips and spoken my love to you, and I've seen your eyes shine brilliantly into mine, and I can die happy now. I can atone for what I've done now that you've granted this wish." I told her the things I wanted to say, and the things I knew I should say. But I was pretending to be more valiant than I was. I wanted more than anything to continue to evade my punishment and stay beside her. I might have stolen, but the dark queen was far from innocent. Our vendetta would never die until she was dead. But now, because of the tangled mess of my past, I was going to lose my future with Celeste.

Hadn't I always known how this would end? Celeste's blue eyes shimmered under my words, and I felt my heart relinquish some guilt and mourning I'd held onto over my decisions. I was wrong — a liar and thief and so much more — but I couldn't regret it at that instant when she looked at me and for a moment, I thought I saw love in her gaze.

"You're not going to die here," she said. My heart hammered in my chest as she walked towards the dark soldiers, power in every move she made.

"Whoever you are, I'm giving you this warning. You are

not in your realm, and you are not dealing with one of your kind. If you don't want to all die, mission further unfulfilled, I suggest you leave. And take your lives as the prize."

"Never. Have him return the item to us," the leader spoke. His eyes were as black as coal, his face as pale and veined as a dead leaf, and his body shook from his contained rage.

She stood in silence for a moment, and I quickly jumped to action, wanting to relieve her from further stress.

"Here," I said, removing the jewel from my ear. "This is what they seek."

Her eyes widened as she took the green stone from my hand. She examined it for a bit, feeling the weight in her hands before she looked at me with hesitation, clearly reflected in her eyes.

"Is it okay if they have this? You said—"

"I know what I said." I paused before making the decision that would set my future, and the fate of my very world, into the hands of fate. "Yes, they can have it."

She debated for a moment longer before she nodded and walked over to the man who led this mission. He was tall and sage. A hardness to his jaw and eyes would have made his face cruel, even if the dark power was not coursing through him. Perhaps that was why he was sent. He offered no mercy.

There would be none given to me, I knew, despite this exchange.

Celeste reached her hands out, poised to hand the jewel over, when his tongue, cursed to spew his ferocity, muttered, "And soon, we will also have his life."

Unwise words from such an intelligent-looking man.

Celeste paused, clenched the jewel in her hand, and slid

it into her jean pocket. The withered soldier watched the movements, eyes burning with hate.

"No, I don't think that will happen. I'm going to hang onto this. Until you can ask nicely." She released her silver ropes of power. "Now leave. And tell whoever sent you that next time, they should send a subordinate whose tongue can negotiate rather than simply anger a god who can only play nice for so long."

Her eyes were alight with challenge. And that foolish, unquenchable man watched with a heated gaze as she walked towards me and the others.

I didn't dare to hope that it would be resolved with such ease, but the closer Celeste came to me, the more my heart shook with relief and joy. Safe. I just needed her safe.

In one instant, so fast I could barely comprehend it, the soldier had sent another spear of power towards her. This attack was large, full of more deadly poison than the last. They might not have been able to kill her before, and most likely never could, but he was giving his all in trying.

I couldn't move. From this distance, even at my top speed, I could never make it; even if my limbs weren't frozen in paralyzing fear.

Celeste met my gaze, steady clarity within her eyes that I'd never seen there before, and she turned, curls bouncing around her heart-shaped face, as she sent a wall of silver light over the soldiers. In an instant they were nothing but sparkling glimmers of fading light. So few creatures could destroy our kind with such ease, but once again, I had forgotten that sweet-faced Celeste was much more than she appeared.

She watched the light fade into the warm afternoon air. Leaving an empty alleyway, looking as though it had never seen a touch of fae magic or the frightening power of a god.

"Celeste, are you—"

"What was that stone to you, Sunny?" Her voice cut through the air and I winced at the power she still carried around her.

Boiling fear shook my body as I formulated a lie. "It is important to me." My wicked heart pounded with a dark vengeance towards the queen that made those words both truth and deception. A greedy triumph sprang inside of me. I still had Celeste. If I said the right thing, only gave enough, maybe I could keep her and continue my plan to end the queen once and for all. "In the dark queen's hands, this is a weapon. I *need* this."

Von stalked to my side, anger radiating off of him in waves. "Really? Do you think for one fucking second I'm supposed to believe you did this for anyone but yourself? That you risked Celeste's fucking life to do what, be a hero?" Von sneered, and for a moment I felt the air shift and I wondered if he would attack.

"She was in no danger!" I yelled, my nerves frayed. "They never attacked in crowds. Only in areas with large amounts of vegetation and few humans. I know them. They couldn't hurt Celeste. They wouldn't hurt people. They only wanted me."

"It looks like they hurt her," G said, his voice hard and dark.

My stomach dropped, my head pounding, my heart aching at his words. "I don't know how. Though the dark guard is more powerful than our previous adversaries, I never thought they would have the ability to affect her. I never meant for this to happen." I looked at Celeste. "I didn't know they'd send such powerful forces for me. In all my years of running, I'd never faced them. I'm so sorry."

Celeste's eyes shimmered with tears as she spoke. "If

you're being honest, if you have that stone because of good intentions, then why couldn't you just explain to me? Why not just say they were after you and why? You said that stone wasn't as important as I was to you. But you risked everything to keep it. I had my life turned upside down because of this secret, so your words couldn't have been true. You're just a liar, Sunny. Everything you've said has been a lie."

This wasn't right. My mind reeled, unsure if keeping my mouth shut would make her hate me less or more.

"It wasn't all a lie. It's not that simple." I told her, equal parts desperate to tell her the entire truth but needing to keep her in the dark. All of this was a calculated risk now. But the one thing I could not risk was losing her. I'd be doing just that if she knew what kind of monster I was. If she understood that the queen wanted me dead because she herself feared me and my power, feared what I could do, what I *did* do. How could I explain that the very stone in her hand was the key to life or death for the people of my realm without telling her more lies? How could I explain that it was the heart of my vengeance without showing her how dark my heart truly was?

"It's never simple," she said softly, cutting off my feeble attempt at words as she tossed the stone back to me. I caught it, despising the thing more than ever. "I hate what I've done here today. I won't do this again."

She turned around, and I watched as she walked away.

The threat was subdued for now, but my shame, and hurt were not so easily dissolved.

Nor was I able to calm my bleeding heart at her next words that she tossed carelessly over her shoulders. "Let's go. I think it's about time I spoke to my mother so we can end this."

It was past sunset, but I didn't have the luxury of caring about my mom's "preferences" and little rules that she demanded to be obeyed by all. I knew one place she frequented right in my little town — in the part of our capital city that housed the most expensive and high-powered citizens. My gut feeling told me she was there, living it up with the rich and powerful. And I didn't even need to use my powers to find her.

I moved on legs that felt stronger than I did inside. I tried to force my body to stop trembling. I cleared my throat and blinked back my tears. I would not go before my mother, weak. But I was hurting.

My mind raced between blaming myself and blaming them. I wanted to regret loving them because it wouldn't hurt so much if I didn't. I was stupid to get so wrapped up in them that I didn't bother finding out if they were people I should love. Even after all of this time, I still didn't know those three as much as I thought. Especially Sunny.

I still didn't know their true character. And I had found mine in an instant.

What I'd done, manifesting that sort of power, was beyond anything I'd ever imagined possible. I'd fought. Attacked. *Taken lives.* No matter that it could be seen as self-defense. There was little someone from their world could do to me that would have actually resulted in my death. They wouldn't have really hurt me. I killed them because I could.

Because I just didn't want to stop and think of any other way. I flexed my fingers, still in disbelief at what I'd done. Still shaking at the hot, racing energy that had come out of my hands; by the words that came out of my mouth. I had never used my powers that way. Since coming to Earth, I had locked most of it away behind clumsy human actions and dimpled smiles, so deeply that I often forgot I was even a goddess at all most days. Now, I couldn't forget.

Like a cosmic puzzle, all moving parts and all mystical veils came together and revealed the truth. I was more god than human. More monster than woman. Because apparently, my self-interest won over everything else every time. Maybe I was more like my mother than I would have ever wanted to admit.

My stomach churned with bile and self-loathing, and I pressed the palms of my hands against my eyelids to stop my tears.

"You can cry sometimes, Celeste. You can't appreciate the good if you ignore the bad."

That's what my father had told me once. I had laughed at him. Thinking wise words didn't quite fit a lovable clown. Now, I wished I could do just that. Cry my eyes out and forget everything that happened over the last few days. I wanted to forget that my carefully constructed mask was cracked, and I was almost torn in two, exposing every weakness I'd ever had.

Worst yet, I was hurt and vulnerable and my mother would latch onto that in an instant.

We walked the long blocks across town in silence. I was glad I decided to hoof it instead of squeezing into a car with those three, where the silence would have eaten me alive. With the sounds of our city buzzing around us, I could focus on my inner turmoil and allow myself to do the one thing I hated most; I stewed in every negative emotion I had.

We all must have had a million thoughts running through our minds as the awkward air of unspoken words suffocated us. Even Von kept his snide remarks to himself, thankfully, as I couldn't bear anymore talking. Any more doubts. I just wanted to be in control of something. This one thing. And since my day was already shit, I might as well pull off the bandaid and get it over with.

My mother's building loomed in the distance and I gulped, my heart doing somersaults in my chest in the nerve-wracking way it always feels when you're about to hit the pavement after a fall or get stabbed by a needle or crash into an immovable force. That tense feeling of dread that numbs your brain and body? Yeah, that's how it felt to even lay eyes on my mom's building.

As if it made any sense, the building looked even more grand and ostentatious than it had when I came here last. My eyes traveled up the glittering glass slides of the building which housed my mother's penthouse. The place was as lux and large as one would expect of a god's dwelling, and my mother made her home at the very top where she could overlook the city and turn her nose down on all the mere mortals down below. Somehow, that included even me.

As we walked up the steps of the apartment complex

that seemed more like a five-star hotel, Von broke our truce of silence and placed his hand on my shoulders. "Are you sure you want to do this?"

I sighed and wilted under his warm hand on my skin.

We had talked about it ad nauseam throughout our time together. Late nights of eating junk food and watching tv had always somehow ended right back to this.

Maybe it wasn't a curse. Maybe I had it all wrong. Maybe I could just forget it, just be with them.

We love you.

But my mind was set. After this afternoon's events, I had no choice.

I nodded at Von, shrugged off his hand, and walked on, taking the elevator up to her private floor.

My mother's butler let us in, a man dressed in barely anything at all save for a bow tie and speedo. My mother was nothing if not a living cliche. A rich beauty wanting to remain rooted in the old world, with men fawning all over her. She got her wish in that department.

As I walked into her home, my line of would-be suitors hot on my heels, I noted the big-screen television and surround sound system. The modern art on the walls, and the bar set up to our right.

I supposed she had no qualms with taking the best of the new world as well.

The butler bowed to us, directing us to where my mother sat in her large, chic office. Floor-to-ceiling windows allowed her the best sight in the city as twinkling lights sparkled like stars over the dark, city landscape. A modern, blooming chandelier of crystal hung over her large, glass desk. In the middle of the room, over the black marble floors was a plush, black and white, fur rug, which very well could have been an entire tiger for all I knew. I rolled my eyes at how she and I were like night and day. Or how I'd always thought so, at least.

My sandals flopped with loud sucking sounds along the floor, breaking the silence with unsophistication. It reminded me of the last time I'd come here; when I thought I could give her a chance. Or rather, thought she'd give me a chance. I pretended to seek out her knowledge, asking a few vague questions about Celora just to spend time with her. She spent so little time with me, even in my youth, but even less so when she found out I had come to the human realm. As always, she shut me down. Asked if I needed money. Threw me a wad of cash and sent me on my way.

I was fifteen and all I'd wanted was my mother. I wanted her affections so badly that I'd dream of her at night. My stomach would twist from longing. I had a wonderful father and a brilliant sister, but I wanted a mother. I got money instead. Gods were horrible parents. At least my dad was a decent fucking person.

I was done with her after that, yet here I was, crawling back to her to seek out her *infinite wisdom*. I knew she would hold it over my head. But I was desperate. And she knew that. Fed on it. My desperation would give her a newfound form of evidence to showcase just how pathetic I was.

I wanted to wring my hands in frustration. I looked around at my stoic entourage. I ignored the beating of my heart when I looked at them. I was guilty of wanting to keep them by my side when I knew I'd end up right in this very spot at the end of it. It didn't matter that I was now a victim of my own poor foresight. I did it to myself.

I was in love with them, but that love alone could never erase the original question.

Why?

What had caused all of this? I had stalled for so long,

taking my sweet time to get to my mother because I didn't really want to hear the answer before.

In doing so, I'd only made it worse.

My mother's back was to us as we walked into her office, but I knew she'd sensed my presence long before. I rested my eyes on the elegant white chair, more like a throne, that overwhelmed her small frame. I could see the glass she swirled in her bejeweled hand. I could see the gentle sway of her foot as she sat there like a bored empress.

"Celeste. It's nice of you to stop by. And what can I do for you this time?" she said, turning to face us finally. I rolled my eyes, disenchanted with her dramatics. The woman knew she was a goddess in every sense of the word.

My mother's brilliant light eyes that were set in a face that the heavens had to have sculptured by hand, met mine. She was gorgeous and with a self-conscious hand, I brushed a loose curl behind my ear, feeling unworthy in her presence. She wore her hair short and slicked back, a sophisticated look that I could never achieve, while her breasts practically popped out of her low-cut top. Her full lips curled into a smile that rose on her face like the sun. I wanted to walk away. I would have. If I had other options.

I straightened my spine. I wasn't a child, and I needed her, whether I wanted to admit it or not.

"Let's not play games, Mother. Why are these men attracted to me like I'm spraying pheromones out of my ass?"

"You're not a very smart girl, are you?" my mother chided. She always did that. She always made me feel stupid. She always told me I was. I guess after a while I believed it. But one thing she wouldn't convince me of was that she was going to get out of this without answering my fucking questions.

"Just tell me. I don't have time for your shit."

"We have all the time in the world." Her grin, the way she knew just why I was there, and still had time to taunt and tease, set fire to my blood.

I stormed over to her desk and snatched her drink out of her hand, throwing the glass to the floor.

"Stop it. Just answer me. For once, just be a fucking mom."

I couldn't stand the amused curl of her lips or the way her eyes took on a shade of pity for my sake. *Poor Celeste,* they screamed. *Poor, stupid Celeste.*

My hands trembled at my side. With just a look, she was shattering my resolve. Standing up to my boss, or demons or dark fairy soldiers was easy. Anything was easier than facing her. Not only was I stupid, but I was also useless, clueless, and I just didn't know how to confront her. Not someone like my mother.

"If you don't tell her what she wants to know, I'll fucking rip your throat out and feed you your windpipes," Von said, suddenly at her side.

I was speechless. I knew he was against me getting answers, so why would he be on my side?

I looked at my mom, whose smile had dropped a notch. She shook her head, standing to her feet slowly. I looked back at Von in fear. "Mom, wait."

"This just won't do," she tsked, throwing her hand out in one sudden move that sent Von crashing into her glass windows and into the world below.

I didn't know I had screamed until the burn in my throat told me so. I didn't know I moved until I was looking fifty stories down, the warm night air whipping curls into my face, my hands crushed into the broken glass of what remained of the window. I strained my eyes to see if I'd find his mangled body on the pavement far below.

"A demon speaking to me that way. Disgusting. Honestly, taking a demon as a lover is rather ridiculous. Even for someone like you," she said before she walked over to me and pulled me away from the window.

"You bitch," I whispered, wanting to attack, to hurt her, even knowing I couldn't take her on. I didn't know what to do because no matter how much rage spun inside of my gut or in my head, the sorrow and grief of what she'd done was stronger. I felt like falling to my knees, ripping myself from her grasp, but I couldn't push her away. I couldn't do anything but let her lead me like I was a lost child.

"Come here." My mom yanked me, dragging me towards the door of her office. "Let's have a drink. I had sworn off killing and here you go forcing my hand. Might as well have cheers to a murder well deserved."

I tore myself from her, moving back towards G and Sunny. I felt warm, reassuring hands on the small of my back, around my shoulders, but I struggled to take comfort in them. One more moment, and I'd be on my knees at her feet, paralyzed from what she'd just done, or rather, what I'd lost.

"Stop being dramatic." She rolled her eyes and went to her bar, dismissing the man candy there, and pouring her own drink.

She shook it in her hand, examined the color, and sipped as if she hadn't just killed one of the men I loved. Bile rose and fell, threatening to spill upon the floor. Something hotter than fire burned in my heart and if I wasn't afraid of what she'd do to Sunny and G, I would try my luck at ripping her apart.

"I like aged liquor. Anything too young, too new, too wet

behind the ears, drives me mad." She tilted the glass my way. "You, for example. Barging in here as if I owe you anything. Did you come here to whine about a curse? Your father might have mentioned that. If I can take anything that man says seriously, of course. But here you are. So what is the problem? Have you suddenly found yourself too desired in this world? Should I cry you a river for having males want to fuck your brains out? Be glad it's so. Based on brains and looks alone, you might have spent your entire life alone," she spat out.

"Celeste, let's go," Sunny said, grabbing onto my elbow. I shook him off.

"You're not saying anything new. You're better than everyone and everything walking the Earth, right? But if that were true, my dad would still love you. If that were true, I—" I wanted to hurt her. Tell her that her little spell didn't work on me, at least. But I was sick. Maybe I wasn't that clever. Because a part of me still admired the bitch. A part of me still loved her with the same foolish admiration I had when I was a young girl, wondering how any woman could be so perfect.

"You know, I knew you were coming, so of course I know why you're here." She sat, crossing her legs on the bar stool as she finished her liquor. "You want to be rid of them, right? I'd especially hope that one." She glanced to my right, and I turned, my heart hammering in my chest as Von appeared, looking a little worse for wear, but he was alive.

"Von! How are you—"

"He's a demon. Not a strong one. Not a very good-looking one. But they can survive a little fall, at least. Had you studied this at all, you'd know a lot more. But no, you wanted to be common, right? Not that you could help it."

"Shut up. Just stop talking bullshit. I just want you to tell me why they're stuck with me."

"Stuck?" she scoffed into her glass. "They aren't."

"Stop lying."

"I have no need to lie. People lie out of fear. I suffer from no such emotion."

My chest clenched. I didn't understand and my mother knew it and loved latching onto any moments of weakness. Her lips curled into another wicked grin. "If you refuse to believe me... then," she shrugged her shoulders. "I'll play along."

"Mother—" I began, confusion clouding my mind. Was she telling the truth or was she just trying to make me feel like I didn't know up from down anymore?

"Here, take this," she said, pulling a glowing vial of gold and silver from thin air. She jiggled it in her hand, and I approached slowly. Was this a solution, or just a cruel joke? I hated not knowing anything. She would never be in this situation. How could it be that I had all of her worse traits and none of the best?

"What is it?" I said, reaching for the small bottle.

"If they truly don't love you, if you have some magnetic power that brought them to your side, then this will give you the answer."

"Really? The answer—"

"Yes."

"And that's it?"

She nodded, a smug smile plastered on her face.

"Th—thank you," I said. I thought she'd send me on a quest to the end of the earth to find it, but here it was. The antidote to some unknown condition that I didn't understand, and as far as she was concerned, I was too ignorant to explain.

"You four run along. The sooner you take it, the better," she warned, and I turned from her, glad to be dismissed from her overpowering presence. I avoided looking at my group as I made my way to the front door, vial firm in hand, and left.

Outside, under the silvery moon and clouded sky, I breathed out a shaky sort of pseudo-relief. I didn't feel as good as I had imagined. But at least I had survived an encounter with her. Now, for the really hard part.

I looked at the glowing vial once again, amazed that this was the answer that I had told myself I so desperately needed. Here it was, in my grasp, but this didn't feel like a victory. This felt like the end.

"Celeste, you don't have to take it," Sunny said. "If this has anything to do with the stone or the dark army, I can—"

"It's not that," I told him. Yes, I was still hurt and confused over that, but as I came face to face with my mother, and all the dreadful ways I'd dealt with my past and origins, I was finding it hard to judge. I also had a feeling that whatever he was keeping from me was something I probably didn't want to know. *Everyone runs away from something.* I just wished I knew what that was, so maybe we both wouldn't have to hurt over it. But this, our last moments together, was no time to dig into it, anyway. There was no more time.

"Then don't take it. Just stay with us." His voice hitched, a plea in his words, in his eyes, that made me want to give in. I was so weak at that moment. I was looking for someone to tell me something that would change my mind.

G remained silent. Always silent, and I was dying to know how he felt. "What do you think, G?"

"Does it matter what I think? You already know how I feel."

He hadn't said he loved me in so many words. Neither had Von. But it couldn't have been more obvious. I knew they loved me, but I didn't know if the doubt they had before was still there or if it was just inside of me.

I looked to Von, who was glaring at the moon as if it was responsible for this.

"Von?"

"I never understood why I wanted you so much," he mumbled. "This would solve that, wouldn't it?"

I nodded. While the other two had entered my life rather content to just get to finally know me, Von had been the main one to come with the question of why. He had accused me of doing something to them. Or at the very least, he thought I could solve the mystery as to why they wanted me. At the time, I agreed with him wholeheartedly. It was odd, and we all deserved answers. The last thing I wanted was a relationship built on something superficial and magical. My mom relied on her godly beauty and appeal to drive her in life. I didn't need to be a goddess to get a man. And I wouldn't let that be the reason I kept them.

"Gods, this isn't as easy as I thought it would be." I let out a hollow chuckle. "But, we're here now. No use turning back. You know... it was nice finally getting to meet you three. It was fun," I said. Throwing them a dimpled smile I knew typically won over hearts.

But they didn't smile back. My eyes burned with miserable, hot tears.

"Can I use your phone, I need to call an Uber," I said to Von.

"Why?"

"I have to go. You know, if I'm going to do this thing, it might be really awkward to break this curse or whatever, staring you dead in the face. And I have some stuff to do anyway," I said.

A glimmer of truth was there. I couldn't do it right that second. I didn't want to lose their love right at that moment. And least of all, right as they looked at me. Right when they realized they never loved me to begin with.

It might have been an awkward four-minute wait time, but I took every second to memorize those final moments I'd have with them. Idle chat ensued as if I weren't ready to throw every beautiful moment we'd had out the window for a sense of certainty that I so desperately needed. And I realized I was desperate then. Desperate to know if I was worth loving by just being myself. With or without the mask. With all the power of the universe at my fingertips or just the charm of my smile, the spark in my spirit.

I'm not sure who broke me the most in those last minutes. I'm not sure it's fair to compare the three-way split my heart broke into, and the impossible number of shards those fractured into.

But there was something so lost in G's gorgeous, soft eyes when he looked at me. In the way, he would almost reach out to touch me, before he would snap his arms back, as if second-guessing if I'd want it, or if he should. I didn't know either. I didn't know if I wanted him to hold me one last time, or if I needed to get used to a life where his large, rough hands weren't caressing my skin. I compromised, grabbing a hold of his hand, and intertwining my fingers with his, running the pad of my finger over the backs of his hands that shook in my grasp.

Sunny, with those pools of tears in his silver eyes, harbored so much emotion there and I couldn't meet his gaze, because if I did, he'd stir up the tears I blinked back. He barely seemed to breathe, tension rolling off of him, fear, anger, so much sorrow that I felt it piercing my heart as he kept his gaze trained on me.

I studied Von. It was easy to do when I didn't have to meet his eyes. When I couldn't, because he was actively avoiding my gaze. The brooding air about him that usually simmered in sensual passion seemed to have evaporated into cold mystery. I couldn't read the frown heavy on his brow, or the laid-back stance he took as he leaned back carelessly against the hood of someone's parked car. I wished I could read his mind. Know if he was eager for me to leave, or desperate for me to stay. If he was tired of fighting for me, literally and figuratively, or if this was hurting him as much as it was tearing at me. I bit my lip, stopping myself from begging him to talk to me and make me feel better about all of this. I knew he saw straight into my selfish nature so he'd know that right down to our last moments together, I still somehow wanted to use him for comfort. Use him for love I was sure I never really earned.

"I mean, now, you can go back to your normal life. I mean, if this thing works," I said, watching another car drive past, knowing any second, it would be the one to take me away from them.

Willingly. I was leaving them, and as much as I wanted to bullshit myself on this one, I knew it was all my choice.

Von's scoff was a familiar catalyst for his biting tongue, as he finally spoke. "Normal. Almost like none of this ever happened?" His deep eyes, fierce and haunting, finally landed on me. "I asked you before if you regretted this. Me, loving you. I think you're finally answering."

Did he think I didn't love him? Didn't fall for them even knowing there was a very real chance they didn't even love me? They might have been hurting, but for all they knew, a simple gulp of this potion would take all their pain away. This was not as easy for me. I was losing *them*.

But it was too late for confessions. They wouldn't mean anything in a few minutes.

"I'm sorry," I told them. *Sorry that I can't tell you you're all I think about now. All I want.*

My chest ached, literal pain gripping me the moment one of the vehicles slowed down to a stop on the curb next to us.

My hands trembled as I opened the door and slid into this stranger's back seat. I looked back, my eyes clouding with pain, fear, and love. The words boiled on my tongue, desperate to hurl themselves at these men, as if it would make a difference. *They should know.*

But I pressed my lips together, stopping myself from making this worse. Again.

I smiled instead. "Goodbye," I said as if I were just bidding goodbye to strangers. My voice was so even, so full of cheer, that I cringed at the sound of it. How could my voice not betray that my heart was breaking into pieces right where they stood?

With a slam of the car door, the car shifted forward down the street and I left behind the three men that had shown me, for the first time in my life, what it had been like to be unconditionally loved.

The car rambled down the dark street towards my home. Soft jazz music played through the speakers and I leaned back in my seat, watching the houses and streetlights as I passed them by. Just a quiet street. Nothing extraordinary, no signs that a pseudo-war had broken out here. No trace of the fact that my life had changed on this very street.

"Have a good night," I called out to the driver that had thankfully left me to my solitude the entire time. I was most likely radiating despair at this point.

Glad I had worn some jeans and sneakers on this particular mission, I looked around with sharp eyes, unsure of what might be watching me from the shadows. Covertly, I slipped into my neighbor's backyard and climbed over their low metal fence. Only knocking over one or two lawn ornaments, I made my way through my backyard and pulled on my back door handle.

I slid the door open with ease. Another, not so smart move on my part, but I locked myself out of my home so many times, I had no choice but to leave myself a little backup entry plan. And it's not like I was really worried about burglars or anything. I chuckled to myself, thinking how stalkers were apparently what I really needed to be on the lookout for. Even so, no matter what happened, I could take care of myself when I had to. I'd found that out the hard way.

I flipped on the lights and smiled.

Well, maybe I needed help sometimes. It sure seemed like someone had come through for me.

The place, my old place, was perfectly normal again. Walls firm. Glass un-shattered. Broken television set and furnishings, all repaired. It was all perfectly the same. But I felt different. Everything about *me* had changed.

In just a few weeks, this place seemed like it wasn't home anymore. I sort of already knew where my actual home was.

I went to my entryway, and on the table was a greeting card. Like something, you'd get from an aisle in a supermarket. Except this one glowed and shone like rays of light were bursting from it.

"Dad," I laughed.

I opened the letter, and a light flashed in my face.

"Your home is all fixed. Neighbors and cops are all taken care of. Make sure you thank me when you see me again. You owe me one! Love you."

I closed the message and watched it disappear.

"Thanks, Dad," I whispered.

I went into my closet, put on my favorite outfit, a long sundress with a cardigan over top. Packed a bag of photos and some of my favorite books. I gently picked up my doll off of my nightstand and shoved my "little Celeste" into my bag as well. My precious thing.

"You're the most precious thing to me, Celeste."

My heart ached as I grabbed my phone off of the coffee table and turned out the lights.

I walked out the door to find my car parked out front. Now that it was operable again, I hopped inside and played my favorite mix of techno and pop, singing along as the wind swept curls along my face and shoulders.

In only a few minutes, I had arrived at the park where I had met Sunny.

I walked to the fountain where I had first seen him glowing like an unbelievably obvious Fae with no concerns other than to be with me.

I giggled out loud. He had stunned me with his good looks and sweet face. He had surprised me with how strong someone could be while maintaining their kind inner beauty.

So much had surprised me and taken me for a wild ride. I had learned so much in just a matter of days. To most gods, it was nothing. No time at all. But for me, a lifetime had passed, growing and learning to love those men every bit as much as they loved me.

Swinging the vial in my hand, I walked towards the little fountain in the middle of the empty park and sat at the edge.

I looked into the water. The streetlights had turned on, and the orange glow reflected in the water below.

Beautiful and dark. Just like Von. I clutched the stone under my fingers, running the tips over the cracked, cold material. G came off so cold initially, but he was so warm and complex inside.

Everything was complex. Life wasn't easy. Von had said as much. But before them, I never really felt that way. I had taken shit from people, but I always just played it off as okay. For the most part, it was okay. Everything was bearable. Nothing ever got into my soul.

But now, everything was battling within my heart. Every fear of losing out on my simple human life. Every hurt over Sunny and the things he never said. Every life I had taken as I managed to explore my power in the most destructive of ways. All of these things were in my soul now, fighting against every ounce of self-preservation I had. Fighting me for dominance and dominion over my future.

It was hard to wear this melancholy around my neck, an accessory, a noose that I'd never had the displeasure of suffering before. I could always find joy in something. But now, my chest ached with the feeling of it, and it was dirty and ugly as it formed a mist of gray to color everything that was once bright. I sent a silent prayer to the heavens, wishing Sunny was here beside me to grant me just one of his infectious smiles. I wished for a lot of things that would never come to be.

But what if they could? Optimism, my old friend, sprang from the dead like a daisy in March, clawing at the recesses of my mind. *Why couldn't they love me? Why couldn't I just believe I was worthy of that?*

"Did you take the potion?"

I jumped, surprised to hear Von's deep, gritty voice cutting into my thoughts. I turned to the three of them, relief and fear bounced around inside of my head. Love overwhelmed my heart.

"What are you doing here?" I asked. "I thought we already said our goodbyes."

Von smirked, but no merriment, even the villainous kind I'd grown to love, sparked in his eyes. "No, that was just an act, Celeste. It was just running out of ways to convince you to stay."

I let out a shaky breath, feeling the tears thicken in my throat. Nothing had changed then. There was no convincing me now.

"So, did you take the potion?" he pressed.

I shook my head. "Not yet."

"Why not?" he asked.

"Well, you know, I was just building up my nerves. My mom could've put some cyanide in here." I smiled, putting the small glowing bottle to my face and shaking it around as if I could examine the contents.

It looked so simple. It was all really simple, actually. I knew that.

"You don't have to take it," he said.

"Von—," I began.

"You know that no matter how we fell, we still fell. Does it matter? Does dumb shit like that really matter to you?"

"What matters is finding out if this was exactly what you feared. Just a curse that a simple potion could break."

"Oh, fuck what I said!" Von snapped. "Fuck all of it. Yes, part of me wants to know why we met the way we did. But you know what, even if that potion did something to me, to us ... I know this feeling is real. I was just being a fucking asshole."

I laughed softly. "I get that. You were being a bit of an asshole. But you didn't push me to find answers. I need to know too, Von. Can't you understand that?"

"But Celeste—"

"Drink it," G said. My eyes popped open in surprise.

"Drink it, and if we didn't love you after, you'd have your answer. Drink."

"What the fuck?" Von yelled, standing up to face G.

"Do you think what she fears is true?" Sunny said quietly, eyes down-turned.

"No, but I think it's fucking useless. I already know the answer. I want her to believe it," Von said.

"She will, after she drinks it," Sunny said, standing.

My heart felt dangerously close to exploding. "Are you sure?"

"Yes," G nodded his encouragement.

Von stood silent for a moment before he replied, his voice low and uneven. "Go ahead, if you need the proof."

I smiled, looking around. I didn't want to do this with them here. But I wasn't sure I'd have the nerve otherwise. Taking a deep breath, I pulled out the stopper, pressed the rim to my lips, and took it down in one huge gulp.

It tasted bitter on my tongue, a bit bubbly and hot. My body warmed as it slid down my throat and I took in a breath, waiting to feel the effects. Waiting to see on their faces if something truly had changed.

Nothing happened.

I looked around at three expectant faces, eyes focused on me.

"Anything?" I asked, wondering if they would feel the effects first.

"No."

"No."

"Sorry, but no."

"You still love me?" I squeaked out, hesitant.

They nodded in affirmation. *Oh, hell no.*

"Mom!" I called out, not caring that humans could be near. Not caring that my shrieks reached out and probably annoyed every other god walking the earth. I wanted answers.

"Shut up, dear. You're embarrassing me."

I whipped around. My mother sauntered towards us, a hip-hugging gown of sequined black adorning her voluptuous frame, a plunging neckline that would make J-Lo blush, showing off her curves, and a string of men beside her as she appeared. She screamed sex and power, and it was enough to make someone want to throw a knife at her.

"Hey, why didn't the elixir do anything?" I asked, my voice rising a few uncontrollable octaves.

Her lips curled into a smile that instantly made me flush with annoyance. "What do you mean?"

"I mean, they're still in love with me." I rolled my eyes to the three men who were standing beside me, looking all manner of confused, amused, and relieved.

"I told you they would be."

"But you gave me the elixir," I said, my voice full of accusation.

"Because you wouldn't stop badgering me. Honestly, you're worse than a child."

"But I don't understand. Wasn't it some magic thing or maybe my abilities that made them want me, I mean, the way you are with men—"

My mother's laughter was pretty, yet somehow cold, and I cringed, waiting for her to finish. "You silly child. You're not me. There is only one goddess of sex and desire and it isn't you," she said, looking me over.

"What? But I thought—"

"Don't think so much. It doesn't suit you."

"You vindictive son of a—"

"Shush or my lips are sealed on this matter."

I hated needing her. I closed my mouth, throwing a glare when I couldn't throw words.

"You don't know by now that a god's power isn't genetic? We gods are created with divine power. Your abilities are your own. Those men didn't love you because you attracted them with some special power. And I or your father would have noticed if someone would have put a spell on you. Only a god would have had the strength to do that. No, these men had no 'magical' pull to you. Well, no more than any lowly creatures would covet after a goddess." She sent them looks of disgust and I made to speak before she stuck her hand up to shut me up.

"No. Let me finish. I have places to be," she continued. "You should have listened to me from the beginning, you arrogant fool. You are a late bloomer. So unaware of your true abilities. In truth, I had placed some magic on you. But its only purpose was to keep any would-be beasts and creatures from the other realms away from you until you reached a more agreeable age. I should've waited to lift the barrier at forty human years, I see."

"Wait, that's why they could suddenly come and actually talk to me on my birthday?"

"Yes. Happy belated birthday, by the way," she said, rubbing her finger under her chin, "But now, I've answered your questions. Satisfied?"

My mouth hung open, about to ask one more thing. But she held up one perfectly dainty finger and spoke.

"Because I know you're curious. The elixir was just a tonic I take to freshen the skin. A little coffee, liquor, and a splash of vodka. Never mind the demon tongue," my mother shot, sly and cool and evil. I was going to have to keep her and Von apart, that was for sure.

"That's it?"

"That's it. Now take care of yourself, Celeste. You'd do well to develop your powers. If one beast can find you—or three—then you have no idea who else can come looking. Get strong, Celeste. You've found yourself in poor company and may well do it again. But I think you know that."

My mother disappeared in a shimmer of light, her group of sex drunk men following behind her.

"Your mother is quite the character," Sunny said.

"I can't believe it. All this time ..." I was more amazed that my mom had actually provided me with exactly what I needed to know. This whole time, I was stressing and hurting for no reason. Never would have pegged myself as that high strung and paranoid. *Yet, here we are.*

"She told you," G said, arms crossed in smug satisfaction. "We told you."

"I know." My eyes watered. So they hadn't found me because of some weird magic thing. They didn't love me as some cruel joke. They saw me through that gut-wrenching imperfection that made me feel like a failure in every single way and found something worthwhile there. They had managed to see past my mistakes, and past the mask I wore, the one that had yet to fully disappear, but that was chipping away every day since I'd met them. For better and for worse. They loved the always late, self-absorbed, man-crazed Celeste, and I had never felt more happy in my life. They were just a group of immortal men that had fallen for me and loved me. For me.

"What are you crying for? I should be the one crying," Von said, sliding next to me.

"You—"

"Yeah, so I guess I had no one to blame but myself. I'm sorry, Celeste. I'd never felt this way before I met you. When I found out what you were, I just assumed... shit. I hoped it was magic. But I guess, it was just my shit. Falling for you like a punk," he said between clenched teeth.

I laughed, wiping away my tears. I threw myself into his arms and hugged him tight. I didn't blame him. We needed to know. We needed to be sure.

I was sure that no matter what this little potion did, I would have still loved them. But now I knew they'd always loved me.

"Come on, my little woman. Let's go," G said, pulling me from Von's arms and picking me up. He carried me bridal style down the walkway.

"No, no. We don't have a home. That old life, it's done. I was getting tired of it anyway and there's only so many years I could keep not aging and get away with it," I smiled.

"Then where to?" Von asked.

"I want to build you a house," G told me. Yes, a huge house, he had said. With enough rooms for an entire army of our kids.

"In the forest?" Sunny asked, hopeful. Yes, with a lavish garden filled to the brim with his favorite flowers, which happened to be mine as well — dahlias.

"I like the city." Von groused. Yes, he loved being able to blend into the shadows and wallow in the dark underground of the human world that reminded him so much of his home.

They were such a handful. Good thing I called the shots around here.

My laughter floated around the park, past the strangers who ran by in the darkness of night, past the trees that swayed and hushed in the light spring breeze.

"No reason we can't do both. We have a lot of time," I said, breathing in a huge gulp of air.

"You sure?" Von asked, ever my little skeptic.

"Oh, I'm sure," I said. "But first, let's find a hotel."

"I like that idea," Sunny said shyly. My little blossoming sex kitten.

"Great. Let's go before we get attacked." I told them.

"Shit," Von grumbled, and I laughed.

Yeah, there was still a bunch of crap we'd have to figure out. And no doubt Sunny's enemies would come seeking my head on a platter someday soon. But I could handle them when it came down to it.

For now, I wanted nothing more than to finally convince this group to give me the four-way I was begging for since day one.

"I'm not touching another man's cock," G had surprisingly objected quite vehemently. Well, who could say what the future might hold?

I never allowed myself to imagine that things would turn out this way; this amazing.

My days just became full of a lot of love, and a crap ton of love-making.

"You three, I haven't said it yet, and I'm sorry for that, but do you know I love you?" I spoke loudly into the night.

"Obviously," Von replied in his arrogant way that made me giggle.

"I love you too," Sunny whispered, and my breath caught in my throat when he did.

"I know," G smiled, rubbing his cheek against me. Oh, my big guy warmed my heart. And they all had my heart.

It was another bout of poor foresight that blinded me to the fact that these three hadn't been the only ones who had fallen in love with me through a weird twist of fate. Once again, I ask, can anything be worse than being desired by a ton of sexy men? A rhetorical question perhaps, but one that did come up as time went on.

But this wasn't a story about that. This was a story of how I first found, loved, and was lucky enough to keep the first three men that had won my heart. No magic needed. No curse befallen on me. I was just a temptress, and a lover, and the luckiest goddamned goddess that has ever lived.

THE END

ACKNOWLEDGMENTS

This is really hard to write, yet so easy to let pour out of me.

Curse of the Laughing Temptress was previously released as an almost standalone novella with honestly, too much fun, and not enough vision behind it.

I was hurt when it wasn't well received, and even more distraught at how much it shook my belief in myself as an author.

But the indie author community is amazing. Truly. At my lowest, authors and readers came out of the woodwork to help pinpoint how I could make my debut novel bigger and better.

Here it is. Long. Strong. Ready to be read all night long.

Thank you to my beta readers and my author friends. You know who you are and I'll spend my life remembering how you pushed me to keep going.

You told me what sucked. You told me what made you laugh. Even those first poor reviews helped shape this book into something better. Thanks everyone who took the time to help this newbie author. So much love to you all.

ABOUT THE AUTHOR

S.Y. Moon is an author of fantasy romance, who spends far too much time thinking and too little time sleeping.

She likes to mix fantasy and realism by creating FMC's with depth, love interests with villainous tendencies and storylines with equal parts soul-shattering love and blush-worthy steam.

She lives with her four kids in Texas, but dreams of living in a mansion on a mountain side, overlooking the sea so she can daydream—and write— in luxury.

You can find her books on amazon

CPSIA information can be obtained
at www.ICGtesting.com
Printed in the USA
LVHW040852180322
713694LV00003B/387